The Story of Peter Looney

The Story of Peter Looney

His year with the Indians

Patricia H. Quinlan

iUniverse, Inc.
New York   Bloomington

The Story of Peter Looney
His year with the Indians

iUniverse books may be ordered through booksellers or by contacting:

iUniverse
1663 Liberty Drive
Bloomington, IN 47403
www.iuniverse.com
1-800-Authors (1-800-288-4677)

ISBN: 978-1-4401-3195-0 (pbk)
ISBN: 978-1-4401-3196-7 (ebk)

Printed in the United States of America

iUniverse rev. date: 3/24/2009

Acknowledgements

This book exists because my mother, Leola Mae Looney Hessom was such a dedicated consistent and detailed researcher of family history. She was the one who discovered the basic story. I am also very grateful to Jo Hordinski, Myra Ellis for reading the entire book, and to Eilene Hogan for her line by line editing. Also, I want to thank the members of my Writers Group at Heather Gardens for their input and encouragement.

Prologue

The story of Peter Looney first came to light when my mother, Leola Mae Looney Hessom retired from government service and spent over twenty years researching family genealogy. She never told me the story. I found it after she died and I began to make sense of the paperwork she left behind.

I found it too compelling to ignore. So my search began for more information. Where was this fort where he was captured? Who was with him? Where did the Indians take them? Why was he singled out to go further north? What did he do while he lived with the Indians?

At times my research brought out more questions than answers. At some point I had to make up my mind how they traveled, what tribe did he live with, and how did he live?

Because all my questions didn't have answers I decided the fiction would have to fill in the gaps.

Chapter I

June 23, 1756

"They mean to kill us, don't they?" Ebenezer Cole sat down next to Peter, sniffling. He'd been sniffling and often muttering to himself ever since their capture almost four hours ago.

Peter shook his head. "If they wanted us dead, we be dead now."

"If they don't want to kill us what will they do?" Cole wiped his nose with the sleeve of his shirt. Peter stared straight ahead rather than look at him. "The little bit of food they gave us cannot sustain us."

Sergeant Peter Looney sat on the dried leaves and pine needles that littered the ground. He leaned against a large log with his legs stretched out and crossed in front of him, resting after a long walk through the woods. Through half opened eyes he studied the Indians who were guarding the seventeen men, three women and four girls being held captive. Every Indian had a rifle in one hand and a tomahawk held close by his belt. Peter suspected they were not all Shawnee.

The Shawnee had been terrorizing the far western frontier of Virginia for over a year. These Indians still wore their red and black war paint, and Peter could see there was still blood drying on a few of the tomahawks. He wondered why they didn't wash it off while they were walking up the creek.

Captain John Smith sat close by propped against a tree. These settlers had looked to him for answers, but what could he say? How could a small fort of seventeen men including one slave hold off a hundred Indians and French soldiers? The loss of four good men saddened him. The loss of his oldest son hurt terribly. It was a wonder no more than four had died.

About ten yards away the four girls and three women huddled together. They didn't know what their futures would be. They didn't know if they even had one. The possible horrors that awaited them left them too devastated to talk, so they hugged each other and cried quietly.

Peter said nothing for a moment, but thought to himself that a long walk through Indian Territory might do Mr. Cole some good. He was too fat as it was.

Cole continued, "Captain Smith says they'll take us to their Indian town. What kind of town could these savages possibly have? Look at them, half naked and all painted up with red and black paint. Why do they do that? I'm terrified enough without them trying to make matters worse. And those French soldiers. Why are they here?"

"Mr. Cole. You talk too much. Stop your simperin and be quiet. They just might shoot ya for sport, just to shut ya up." Peter stood up and walked back and forth within the tight confines of the camp. His hands were tied in front of him as were the other captives. He wanted to be away from Ebenezer Cole. The fat, little, bald man had made him angry but he walked back toward Cole, who sat with his knees pulled up to his chin. Peter leaned forward and whispered, "If what I know about the Shawnee be true, your life be a short one. You best pray the end be quick, and painless, though I doubt that be so." Cole's eyes flew open wide and he let out a sickening screech that penetrated the quiet of the forest. The Indians glared at him and one raised his tomahawk threateningly. Cole quickly shut up and said no more.

Food that the Indians stole from the fort had been doled out; cold boiled beef and cold greasy fried corn cakes. It wasn't half enough for sixty-seven Indians, three Frenchmen and twenty-four captives, but it would have to do.

Peter removed his boots to allow his feet to dry and air out after miles of treading through a creek bed. He held them loosely across his chest, and lay down on a bed of dry leaves and pine needles to sleep. "God in Heaven. I thank ya for soft dry pine needles and the clear open sky. Amen." There had been no campfire and no way to treat the wounds he and the two Robinson brothers suffered during the battle that day at Fort Vause.

As he slept the battle replayed and he heard the yelling, the screaming and the rifle blasts. He heard the bone chilling war cry of the Shawnee, and the screams of the women and girls as the Indians over ran the small fort."

The day had begun peacefully. The militiamen inside the fort were aware that Indians had been watching the fort for the past few days. Captain John Smith had received word from Governor Dinwiddie that he had no men available to send to Fort Vause. When the guards at the palisade spotted two white men running toward the fort they called down for the gate to be opened. As the gate was unlocked the Indians stormed into the fort with their war cries filling the air. The two white men were the first to die as the Indians overran them.

Arrows whistled through the air, and musket fire exploded. There was no time for a command. Captain Smith had been inside the Vause house writing yet another letter asking for re-enforcements. As the yelling and shooting began he knocked over the small table and grabbed his rifle.

Mrs. Vause stood in the doorway of her house with one of her daughters. "What's happening?" she shouted. "Oh, dear God in Heaven!" The sudden realization left her paralyzed. Peter ran as fast as he could and pushed them into the house knocking them onto the floor. He bolted the door seconds before a musket ball pounded into the heavy log frame.

Captain Smith propped the barrel of his rifle onto the nearest window sill and shouted over his shoulder. "Keep down. Cover that window. Charlotte, get more lead balls. More powder. Reload these muskets. Tom, take this rifle and cover that window over there." He yelled as he tossed a rifle to Mrs. Vause's slave.

The Shawnee war cry was an ear piercing, high pitched, gut wrenching scream that sent shivers up and down every spine. Fear gripped their stomachs, especially the women and girls who had never experienced such a violent attack. There were close to a hundred Indians outside, all of them running and yelling as they fired muskets and shot arrows. The thud against the heavy log walls of the house continued. It was bang, thud, bang, and thud. Peter watched in horror as Captain Smith's son,

Lieutenant John Smith, fell to the ground with blood gushing from his throat. He was quickly scalped. In that moment Peter felt a bullet fly past. Jessica screamed. He recovered quickly and shot the Indian. Lieutenant Smith's scalp fell to the ground but another picked it up. An ear perching war cry appeared at Peter's side and he grabbed another musket. He fired and another Indian fell. There seemed to be no end to the screaming and the shooting. The air in the house grew stifling. Sweat poured from every scalp. The smell of gun powder filled their noses and blurred their vision. Throats were dry, but there was no time for a sip of water. There hadn't been a break since ten o'clock that morning.

Six year old Sarah Medley sat on the floor in the corner with her hands over her ears, screaming and crying. There was no one to comfort her.

Mrs. Vause's Negro slave and Scottish servant girl were at one window. Captain Smith stood at another with Levisa Vause reloading as quickly as she could. Peter Looney was at a third with Charlotte Vause reloading his rifle. Peter felt the wind as musket balls flew past him. Another sent splinters of wood flying into his face barely missing his eye.

"Jessica. I need more lead balls," yelled Captain Smith.

"Jessica. Bring me more powder. Hurry, I'm almost out," called Peter.

From the window Peter caught the acrid smell of smoke as it entered his lungs. From the corner of his eye he saw red flames rising through the black smoke that curled into the blue sky. Flames erupted from the other buildings within the fort's walls. Smoke drifted into his nose, eyes and mouth. He continued to fire and blinking his eyes as they kept tearing up. He fired with less accuracy, but with so many Indians running around his musket balls usually found a target.

A tomahawk appeared at the window, welded by a strong, brown arm. Peter barely avoided its blade as he pointed the barrel of his rifle into the face of the Indian and pulled the trigger. Charlotte's ear splitting scream was so close it seemed to come from inside his head.

The Shawnee continued their war cry for as long as the battle continued. Peter's ears rang from the noise of his own musket. Even Mrs. Vause's Negro slave and servant girl did their best in the battle, but by four o'clock in the afternoon everything changed.

"Captain Smith. The back wall is on fire." Jessica called frantically.

"Don't let it get to the powder. It looks like we'll have to surrender. No re-enforcements are coming. We have no choice but to surrender." He opened the door and threw his musket onto the ground. Then he and the others walked out with their hands held high. Little Sarah clung to her mother's skirt.

Thomas Robinson and the rest of the men walked slowly through the fort when they saw Captain Smith with his hands up. They had been scattered throughout the fort and now realized that he was surrendering. They came forward with their hands held high. "They got John." He looked sympathetically at Mary Ingles.

When Mary heard that her husband, John was dead, she collapsed.

Peter bent over and pulled Mary to her feet. "Stand up Mary. That's a good girl." She did as he asked but she shook as if she were freezing even though the day was very hot, and tears ran down her cheeks blinding her to everything around her. He kept his arm around her.

The French soldiers, who had joined with the Indians in the raid, tied each person's hands in front of them and then ran a rope from one to another so they were all tied together. Peter's shoulder was red hot with pain from the musket ball that barely missed his shoulder bone. He bit his lower lip rather than make any noise as they tied his hands and pushed him with the others. He looked around while the Indians removed their dead. There were thirty-two Indians plus two dead French soldiers. Among the settlers three had died along with John Ingles. Those captured were Mrs. Vause and her two daughters, Captain John Smith, William Bratton, Joseph Smith, William Pepper, Ivan Medley and his two daughters, John Walker, Ebenezer Cole, Jonathon Graham, James Bell, and Tom, a slave and Sally, a servant girl.[1]

Peter woke in a cold sweat, with the sound of musket shots ringing in his ears. He hoped he hadn't cried out as he sat up and looked around. There was no moon and all he could see were stars overhead. He listened intently. The woods were ink black and high in the sky the twinkling stars shone like diamonds. The quiet was as deafening as the Shawnee war cry had been loud. He lay back down and waited for his heart to stop pounding. Presently a twig broke. A leaf rustled against other leaves and something scrapped against the bark of a tree. The gentle gait of four small hooves bounded into the blackness and Peter realized a deer had wandered close to camp.

Captain Smith was also awake. He too had been listening to the silence of the night and heard the deer approach. He tried to focus his attention on the deer's gentle steps. His tormented brain had been reliving the gruesome sight of his son's mangled and scalped body lying on the ground. *Thank God, his mother wasn't there to see it.* He felt that the governor had let the settlers down, and by association he had let them down. How could an officer protect the frontier with so many Indians raiding the settlements, and being led on and paid off by the French?

The Indians had taken four scalps and looked at the others with a menacing and hungry eye. Their thirst for blood was only partially satisfied, but they obeyed their Chief Gray Fox. The captives had been marched into the woods while cattle and some of the horses were slaughtered. The three women and four girls were allowed to ride on the few horses they brought back. The girls doubled up, riding bareback. They had no saddle blankets, just the hot backs of the horses on which they rode. Jessica rode behind her sister, Sarah. Levisa rode behind Charlotte. An Indian took the rein and pulled the horse along as the girls and women held onto the horses' manes as best they could. All the white men were required to walk as did some of the Indians.

Once assembled in the woods, the chief and Captain Babbee led the party of sixty-seven Indians, three Frenchmen, and twenty-four captives into a small creek where their tracks would be hidden. They walked through the water from one creek to another, and then left it to climb up a ridge, one hundred feet above. Boulders and thick underbrush made the climb difficult. They held up their bound hands to keep the branches from stinging their faces and necks.

They followed ravines and crossed ridges, always in dense forest. Their general direction was west away from the fort and they passed a few miles south of Draper's Meadow.[2] They turned northwest and climbed a ridge to the top of Price Mountain and there the Indians stopped. That first night they ate only what little food had been in the fort. With no fire the greasy food had to be eaten cold.

The sky turned gray and the stars faded away as dawn approached.

"Sounds like a whippoorwill." William Bratton had crept close to Peter during the night.

"That ain't no whippoorwill, Billy. Did you ever hear a whippoorwill in the morning? They do their singin' at night. That's the Indians. They're probably lookouts in case somebody tries to follow us."

"Who's gonna follow us? Once they see all these Indians they'd surely give up."

"I don't know. For the sake of the women and girls I hope we get found."

Everyone began to rise as a red glow appeared low on the eastern horizon. The Indians gathered the horses that had been hobbled for the night. The captives rose and moved behind trees to relieve themselves.

"Sergeant Looney, what are we to do about food?"

"Mr. Cole. Didn't you eat a piece of meat and a corn cake last night?" Peter looked at Mr. Cole, somewhat irritated. *Why ask me?*

"But, that was food they stole from us."

Peter shrugged and started to walk away, "There ain't no food for us this mornin'. Maybe we'll eat tonight."

"But, we can't walk all day on empty stomachs. Mine is already making noises, telling me I need to eat."

Peter was angry now. "Go complain to the Indian Chief. Maybe he can do something. As for your stomach, Mr. Cole. It'll just have to keep on growlin'." Ebeneezer Cole walked away grumbling to himself.

William Robinson ripped the sleeve from his shirt and tied it around his neck wound to stop the bleeding. His brother, Thomas, had a knife wound in his ribs and a cut on his head. The blood had dried somewhat but as he rose to his feet the cut in his ribs began to ooze a little more blood. Neither man uttered a word of complaint.

Until yesterday Fort Vause and Fort Preston were the two forts that stood at the far edge of the western settlements between the Allegany Mountains and The Blue Ridge. With no funds from the governor, Ephraim Vause used his own money to build a fort around his house and a few buildings. Now, as the captives prepared to continue their journey deeper into Indian Territory, Peter reflected on the past events and hoped that Vause would pick up their trail and follow.

Peter was the tenth of thirteen children and possessed a fairly jovial sense of humor that he shared with the rest of his family. His father had been one of the first to settle in the area just south of the James River, and they had lived there since 1742. They were a prominent family in the expanding community. Peter had two hundred-fifty acres on Craig's Creek and he was only twenty-two years old.

"Come on, Cole. Get up and come along. We've got a mighty long journey ahead of us."

"Sergeant Looney?"

"Yes, Captain Smith."

"What do you know about this?"

"I doubt I know any more than you do, Captain. I've known some Cherokee since I was little. Most of these are Shawnee and their towns are north of the Ohio."

"Yes, I know. Well, I hope my boots hold up."

Chapter II

"Mr. Vause, there's a rider coming this way, and he's movin' mighty fast from the looks of that cloud o' dust he's stirrin' up."

"Oh, my god. I hope all's well at the fort."

Ephraim Vause, and four friends were two miles from his fort and home. They had been leisurely walking their horses to give them a little rest in the afternoon heat. "That man's ridin' hard. Look at how he beats the sides of that poor horse."

"I pray it's not Indians." Ephraim Vause hurried to meet the messenger.

The man pulled his horse to a sudden stop when he drew near. "Mr. Vause. Mr. Vause," he called. "Oh, Lord help us. It's Indians. They're burnin' everythin' in the fort."

"Where's my family?" Vause answered in alarm.

"I don't know! I didn't dare get too close. They be shootin' and yellin' somethin' fierce. They're all inside the fort. The Indians. Oh Lordy! I fear all is lost."

"Oh my God! My family!" Ephraim Vause didn't wait to hear the rest of the message. He had already kicked the heel of his boot into the side of his horse. It reared up onto its hind legs with a whinny and leaped into a gallop. In no time the others hurried to catch up. By the time Vause reached the fort smoke hung in the air overhead; a dark gray cloud covered everything within the fort. White ash rained on

9

him like warm snowflakes. Everything that had not already burned was still engulfed in flames. The sickening sight and smell of dead cattle, and dead horses baking in the afternoon heat, littered the ground and field beside the fort. Four bodies lay inside the walls, butchered so badly it was almost impossible to identify them. As they walked among the hot coals and ashes it was what he didn't see that gave Vause cause to hope. His wife and daughters were not among the dead. They had to still be alive.

"What do you reckon we ought a do Ephraim?" Josh Miller asked.

"We'll follow. We'll form a party. Round up as many men as you can and meet me back here. They have to have left a trail. Look here." Ephraim picked up something small and shiny from the ground. "Looks like a uniform button. French. I'll bet they're behind this."

"We got to bury these poor souls first."

Each man rode out to make sure his own family was safe, and to bring shovels and provisions for a long trip. After checking on their families they each rode out to their neighbors to recruit men for a rescue party.

"Most of the people around here have already left or they're packin' up their wagons. They mean to quit this place and go east where it's safer. Matthew Harmon here done sent his wife and children with his brother. Abraham and me told our families to pack a wagon and go to family in the east. We'll catch up to them later. Bobbie Tracy ain't got no family, just his self."

"My brother was one of those at the fort. I be wonderin' if he was a prisoner."

"I'm sorry, Bobbie, but he was one of those we just buried."

"Oh no." He hung his head as he fought back the tears. "Then . . . I . . . I be ridin' with you, Sir."

"I thank you, Bobbie." Vause put a hand on his shoulder. "We need every man we can get."

By the time the men returned with supplies for the journey the day was long gone and the sun had set. Their party numbered thirty four men; each with a horse and rifle. "We'll have to camp here tonight and start out at first light. Did anybody bring food?"

"Mr. Vause. I got a ham my neighbor done give me. He had it

hanging in his smoke house and said he couldn't take it with him when he left."

"Thank you, Timmy. We'll be most appreciative."

Later that night they lay on their bedrolls and listened as Ephraim Vause said a prayer. "Dear Lord. We thank you for the fine ham that Timmy Motes brought us, but we ask that you take care of our friends and family members who have been captured, and please look over their safety, wherever they be. Amen."

First thing in the morning the men were eager to start out. In the woods they found graves and many tracks of both men and horses. "The women must be on horseback. I don't find any small prints leaving from here. But, there were several leading up to here." They followed the tracks to the river.

"Well, it looks like they traveled up the creek to hide their tracks. Most of them seem to be on foot, some boot prints and lots of moccasins. They all stopped at the creek."

"If most of them are on foot it shouldn't be too hard to track 'em."

"Yes, sir."

Chapter III

There was no water on the top of the mountain. The warriors that had disappeared the evening before returned. The horses were brought up to the camp, and those who had ridden the day before re-mounted. The column proceeded down the northwest side of the mountain to another creek.

Peter approached Sarah. "Drink as much as you can hold. It will help ease the pains of hunger." She turned her little face up to look at Peter and he saw her eyes begin to water. "We'll eat today, little one. I'm certain of it." She turned away with an expression of distrust. She knew Peter only slightly and though he was kind she had been too terrified the day before to trust anyone now.

They followed the creek where it flowed into the New River and turned north. The New River was too wide to wade, so they traveled along its bank. Many times they climbed and followed along smaller creeks away from the river before they found convenient fording spots, and then followed the same creeks back toward the New River. With every creek too deep to walk across they were forced to make a detour. Indian scouts were out to make sure they were not being followed, and also to hunt for the food they would need.

Peter and Captain Smith were independently praying that Ephraim Vause was a good tracker. The New River was seldom out of sight for more than an hour as they detoured up and down the feeder creeks.

The overall topography was rough with steep hills and dense forests that cut their visibility and slowed their progress.

Peter wondered what other tribes had joined the Shawnee. He knew the Cherokee but also knew that they were enemies of the Shawnee. He was also too far back along the line to hear anything said between Chief Gray Fox and the French Captain. Each captive had an Indian guard watching him so Peter couldn't talk to anyone. There wasn't much to say anyway, and he was glad he didn't have to listen to Mr. Cole's whimpering. Then he thought about Jessica Medley's long red hair and noticed that it glowed brightly whenever it was touched by the sun. It was a beacon that called to him and his one source of pleasure as they all trudged through the forest over beds of rotten leaves, pine needles, loose rocks and dead branches.

All the second day they followed the course of the New River. Peter's arm continued to burn. The musket ball passed through and he would at least not have to worry about removing a lead ball. He just hoped the wound wouldn't fester.

The river turned a sharp bend exposing a sand bar large enough for all of them to gather. Here they were allowed to rest a moment and drink water. By noon the air was very warm and still even in the forest. The water felt cool and Peter tried to use his hands to put some on his burning shoulder, but with both hands bound together that was impossible. He walked a few feet into the river where it came up to his thighs and leaning his shoulder into it was able to cool the wound. He stayed that way letting the water wash over his shoulder until he was pulled back by one of the warriors.

The topography grew still rougher as they wound their way deeper into the mountains. They left the river and climbed up into the brush and trees. The path they followed rose over fifty feet above the water.

"What's that noise?" Sarah asked suddenly.

"It's a waterfall. Sounds like a big one." Levisa turned her head to look back at Sarah.

Then through a break in the trees, Sarah exclaimed, "Wow. Look at that. Can we go down there?"

"Sarah, hush." Jessica demanded. "Be quiet."

"That be a big one alright," Peter said.

It was a raging torrent at least twenty feet high and just as wide.

They continued along the edge of the river, still far above it, but near enough that Peter found the view pleasing in spite of his weariness. Boulders the size of a cabin began to block their way in places and they had to climb still higher to go around them. Each boulder slowed their progress, as did the deeper streams. On the other side of the ravines they followed the same creek back down to the upper side of the waterfall. Within two miles they came to another smaller waterfall.

Jessica's red hair continued to attract Peter's attention. Her cap had fallen off when the Indians pulled her into the woods. There was nothing to keep it in place so it swayed back and forth as the horse moved and the occasional breeze blew it aside. As Peter focused his attention on her hair he began to wonder about the girl. She was pretty, or so he thought, with freckles sprinkled across her nose. He had only spoken a few words to her before the attack, and hoped he would have an opportunity to speak to her again. Then he tripped on a rock.

"Damn," he exclaimed. *I must be daft. I be thinkin' crazy thoughts this day. We don't know what be our fates at the end o' this trail, if we even be gettin' to the end. But, why keep us alive only to kill us later? Now, that's what I be thinkin'.*

Again they left the river and climbed two hundred feet up another mountain. Such a stiff climb had the girls holding tight to the horses' manes whose hooves were slipping on the loose rock and soil. There were more boulders to navigate, and by the time the sun set and night approached they finally reached the top, exhausted.

Tonight the Indians built a fire and untied the captives. Some of the warriors disappeared as others kept watch over them. In the distance Peter heard the crack of a rifle, then another, then a third. "Three shots. I hope that's game they be shootin', and I hope they get some." Before too long, three warriors approached carrying a deer and two turkeys. A second fire was built. Peter watched as they began butchering the deer, saving the skin. Before long deer meat was sizzling over one of the fires and the plucked turkeys over the other one.

The Chief carried a skin bucket of water to the larger fire and dropped hot rocks into it. When the water began to boil he added a few green leaves. Peter watched in confusion. "Now, what would he be doin' with that mess? Surely, he don't expect us to eat it."

The captives were allowed to move around as long as they stayed within the circle of the camp. Peter ventured closer to Jessica. "Miss Medley. How are ya holdin up?"

"I'm tired. Thank you for asking, Mr. Looney."

Jessica looked away from Peter. In addition to being tired, she had never spent so much time on a horse and was sore in places she couldn't mention. Her dress was a little dirty and the hem was torn in a few places. Her feet and ankles were scratched from the brambles and bushes. She had been barefoot when the Indians invaded the fort. Shoes were difficult to obtain and to save what they had children and some women went barefoot around the house. Her red hair was hanging in loose strands. Jessica was the kind of girl who took pride in the way she looked and was embarrassed at the way she imagined herself. She was also a bit angry, but she didn't know exactly where she could direct that anger. The Indians would probably kill her rather than put up with her, so she didn't dare complain to them. As for the others, there was really nothing any of them could do. At least she didn't have to walk, and Sarah was easy enough to deal with.

Peter knelt down on one knee in front of her and said, "If I can do anything for ya, I'll try. Don't know how much they'll allow."

"That's mighty kind of you. Captain Smith has made the same offer. It's good to know we have friends though we are surrounded by all these savages." A tear ran down her face and she brushed it aside. Her sister, Sarah, sat down next to her and wrapped her little arms around Jessica's waist and buried her head in Jessica's breast.

"Don't cry, Sarah." Peter reached out one hand and touched her arm. "You must be a brave lassie. The Indians will think more kindly towards ya."

"I'm trying, but I want my mamma."

"Sure ya do. I imagine your sister does too, but you gotta be brave. Your Pa be close by."

"Yes." Sarah grabbed the hem of her dress and wiped her eyes.

Peter walked a few feet away and sat down next to Ivan Medley. "Your girls be tryin' their best to be brave."

"Yes. I don't know what to say to them. Their Ma died this past winter." Ivan sat with his arms around his knees and leaned his chin on one knee. "Their Ma knew how to talk to them. Guess I'm not too good at that."

"Just havin' ya close by with a gentle arm would be a big help. Sarah could be braver if you show her you're up to the task as well. Don't mean to preach, but . . . ."

"Then don't. I'll take care of my own." He scowled avoiding Peter's eyes. Peter walked back to the other men.

A few minutes later Chief Gray Fox approached Peter with something in his hands. "You sit." When Peter sat down the Chief ripped the sleeve from Peter's shirt.

"Hey, what are ya doin? This be my good shirt."

"You be quiet." The chief did not sound angry, but firm.

He spread a warm, dark green and mushy substance over Peter's wound and wrapped his arm with the sleeve from his shirt. Then the Chief stood up and looked at him intently, "You be better soon." He turned and walked over to the Robinson brothers and did the same to their wounds.

After everyone ate, leather skins filled with water were brought from the creek and each person was given a drink. The camp grew quiet as the captives lay down on the leaf covered ground and fell asleep. Somewhere in the distance an owl hooted.

Peter woke suddenly, and though he didn't move, he opened his eyes. The faint gray of pre-dawn was visible in the sky. The warriors were on the move bringing the horses back from where they had been hobbled. Their hoof steps created just the faintest vibrations of the ground, but Peter felt it.

The entire party was on the move again. They continued to follow the same river, detouring up and down feeder creeks and ravines too hazardous to cross lower down. The detours seemed to take a long time, slowing their overall progress.

Peter heard the scream of a horse in pain. He turned to see a warrior jump lightly to the ground. His horse continued his heart breaking scream. *Such pain. That poor horse.* One leg had broken on the boulder lined ravine. *Too bad the Indian didn't break his fool neck.* But, the Indian got up and calmly shot the horse. *At least the poor animal is out of his misery.* The sharp ring of the musket penetrated the silence of the forest and the echoes faded away across the mountains to silence again. The Indian said nothing and continued on foot.

That afternoon a summer thunderstorm covered the mountains,

causing the creeks and rivers to rise. The column of Indians and captives continued on. The light cotton dresses, worn by the girls and women, were easily soaked through and their hair hung in wet strands. The men's shirts and pants were also soaked. Moccasins and boots became soggy. The only ones who didn't seem to mind the weather were the Indians. The French had their wool uniforms, and though they were drenched, the wool kept them warm.

The group stopped early for the night, but the fire built by the Indians was not enough to warm anyone. Clouds hung low obscuring the tops of the mountains. Fog closed in around them making visibility difficult. The meat brought in by the hunters was cooked and each one had something hot to eat. Wet wood created so much smoke that those standing near the fire were rewarded with coughing spells. The captives huddled together under the trees to keep warm.

Ivan Medley barely looked at his two daughters; he stared straight ahead with eyes unfocused. With his graying hair untied and his beard so full he was a menacing sight. Jessica Medley was barely able to reach him. "Father." She shook his shoulder. "Father, would you please help me keep Sarah warm? Keep her close and put your arms around her." Jessica removed her apron and wrapped it around Sarah's shoulders. Even wet it was something. She looked at Sarah's blue lips and shivering body.

Without answering, Medley wrapped an arm around Sarah and they warmed each other. The three of them leaned against the trunk of a large tree where less rain filtered through.

Peter spent the night under another tree covered by leaves he had piled over himself. Even wet leaves and tiny branches made enough of a blanket that he slept soundly. When he woke the next morning he saw little Sarah snuggled up against her father. "Poor little lassie," he whispered.

People began rising, but the night had not been enough to dry their clothing, and they shivered in an early dawn breeze. Again, the Indians seemed to be the least affected by the weather as they gathered the horses.

"I barely slept a wink all night. I thought I'd freeze in these wet things," Sally complained. She was Mrs. Vause's servant, but on the trail she ignored Mrs. Vause and stayed away from her. She sat next to Tom, the slave, and looked defiantly at Mrs. Vause.

"I reckon as how, we'll warm up plenty soon as we get movin' and the sun gets up." Tom looked at Sally and she smiled weakly in response.

Their tracks had been washed out the evening before, but Levisa wasn't about to let that hamper the rescue party she felt certain was coming. "Charlotte. Will you come with me, please?"

"What is it?" Levisa was three years older than her sister, but they had always been close. Charlotte followed her to the edge of the creek where a large sycamore tree stood majestically clinging to the edge of the bank.

"Just stand there on that side of the tree and watch that Frenchman doesn't see what I'm doing."

Charlotte whispered. "Okay, but what are you doing?"

"I picked up a piece of charcoal from the fire. I'm going to write my name on this tree. Maybe, father will see it and know that we're still alive, and that he's found the right path. I'm going to squat so they'll think I'm doing my business. Turn around so you can't see what I'm doing."

Charlotte pulled her skirt out to help hide her sister. "Be careful. I hate to think what they will do if they realize what you're up to."

"I know, but I have to do something, especially since the rain washed our tracks away. I'll keep this piece of charcoal in my pocket and use it whenever I get a chance. There, I'm done. We'd best get back to the others."

"Yes. I want to see to Sarah. Her father was with her, but he doesn't seem to be quite right."

"Why? I haven't heard a word of complaint from him about anything."

"That's part of what concerns me. He never says anything. I'm afraid that he's not quite right in his mind. He kept Sarah warm last night, but still I worry. He used to be full of fun before his wife died. Now, he seems too sad for words."

"Charlotte. Sweet concerned Charlotte." Levisa put her arm around her sister. "You seem to take on everyone's problems. But, I fear you will make yourself ill."

Chapter IV

Flies multiplied and the heat rose steadily. Their clothing barely had time to dry before it began to soak up sweat as the captives walked or rode through the hot steamy afternoon along the river. One discomfort replaced another and the party of Indians with their twenty-four captives still had not crossed the mountains. The men were free to walk side by side where ever the heavily forested trail permitted.

Jessica Medley tried to break a branch to swat the flies, but every time she reached for one she would bend it just as her horse pulled away. Peter broke a branch and handed it up to her, then walked beside her horse.

"Thank you, Mr. Looney. You are most kind."

"Please, call me Peter. Would ya mind if I called ya Jessica?"

"I don't see why not. I'm certainly in no mood to fall on etiquette in this horrible place."

Peter smiled. "You think it horrible, do ya? There is much beauty in these mountains. The hills be different shades of blue and green. And such a variety of trees have ya never seen afore? Why each has a different shape and shade of green. Then the birds entertain . . . ."

"How can you possibly think this place beautiful when we are suffering so greatly? I've had nothing but a few bites to eat, and nothing so far today. I shall be skin and bones before long, and be old and wrinkled before we are returned home, if ever. Did you know that when Mary Ingles returned from her being captured last year, her hair was as white as snow? And her not yet twenty-five. You can ask Mary. She's her sister-in-law. She'll tell you." She shed tears as she whined, but little Sarah sitting in front of her on the same horse looked at Peter and smiled.

"I do apologize, Miss Medley. I reckon we have differing points of view on the subject." Peter turned away and stepped back to follow. He looked at the river and paid less attention to Jessica. Suddenly the pretty girl with red hair seemed shallow and spoiled. He had admired her beauty, but was now seeing another side of her. Maybe that was all there was, like a beautiful porcelain doll; just something pretty to look at. And what about Sarah? Didn't Jessica care about her little sister? Of the two Peter was certain Sarah was the stronger in spite of being only six. Sarah had turned and smiled at Peter but said nothing.

Levisa rode with her sister, Charlotte, but neither of them said much to anyone but each other. "Charlotte, that last creek ran from the west didn't it?" She whispered to her sister.

"I think that makes six so far that come in from that direction, but most notable are the turns in the river, and the high banks of each side."

"We must remember, especially if we move away from this river. Would you say our general direction is northwest?"

"Yes. I think so. It's so confusing when the river bends so much. I think the waterfalls will be easier to remember."

"We must also remember that we are going upriver, everywhere we go."

The gap between the mountains on either side of the river grew tighter and steeper. They climbed even higher up the side of the mountain. Smaller rocks broke loose and tumbled down the mountain side. At times these rocks fell free for a hundred feet or more before splashing into the river below. At other times they seemed to never reach the bottom; so far and too small to make any noise over the roar of the waterfall.

"Be careful girls. The horse will find his way. You don't want him to stumble on these loose rocks." Peter was following behind the horse that Jessica and Sarah were riding.

Jessica replied, "This silly horse wouldn't know a rock from a mud hole."

"Just the same, be careful."

"If I don't hold on I'll slide off his backside." Jessica complained and Sarah giggled.

"Oh, shut up Sarah. You think everything is funny. Just you wait 'til we get to their village or town or whatever it is. You won't be finding anything to laugh about."

Late in the afternoon, they slowly made their way down the steep mountainside and through the brambles to the river bed. At the inside of the bend was a wide sand bar. The water was calm and wide, and there were two small islands in the center.

"This is a lovely spot," exclaimed Mrs. Vause. It would be nice to stop here and cool off in the water. It's so hot today." She wiped the sweat from her forehead with her hand, but it did little good. "This must be the hottest summer I've seen in many years."

The chief heard her but he ignored her and led the party into the water that was no deeper than to the rider's knees. For those on foot the water reached their chest.

Levisa looked around her. They were on the western side of one mountain but following Wolf Creek upstream, and to the west. "We aren't stopping and I need to leave a clue," she whispered to Charlotte.

"So drop something."

"Yes. The hem of my skirt is already a bit ragged, but I can't reach it without drawing attention. Maybe this blue ribbon from my chemise." She pulled at the ribbon and bit it with her teeth. It came apart easily and she let it fall to the ground. "I hope the savages don't see it."

Peter noticed her pulling on some part of her dress and wondered what she was doing, so when he saw the piece of ribbon fall to the ground, he stepped on it to make it a little less obvious to the Indians. He turned to look at the warriors behind him. They were all looking up, so he breathed a sigh of relief. *We be leavin' a good enough trail and if it don't rain again, we be easy to follow.*

Whenever Peter looked behind he noticed that Mr. Graham was having trouble keeping up. Peter and many of the other men were backwoodsmen, and accustomed to long treks, but Mr. Graham was a good twenty years older and not in great shape to start with. He lagged further and further behind and the Indian nearest him kept prodding him to move faster. He staggered and tripped over stones. The Indian pulled him to his feet and kicked him.

Finally, he gave up and lay down in the middle of the trail. "I can't go no more." He took a deep breath. "Let me be." He was breathing so heavily he could barely speak.

The Indian next to him kicked him again and repeated his demands in Shawnee. Graham didn't know what he said but his intention was obvious as he continued to kick him. Chief Gray Fox turned at the sharp voice of one of his warriors and rode back to where Mr. Graham lay on the ground.

"You get up and walk. We not stop here," he ordered.

"I can't go on. Let me be. Let me be," Graham begged and covered his head with his arm to ward off further blows.

Tom turned and feeling sorry for the man offered, "I help him walk."

"No." Demanded Gray Fox. "He not get help. He slow down all. You go." He motioned for Tom to continue up the trail. Then Gray Fox said something in Shawnee and rode back to the head of the procession. The rest of the party moved on and once the last one was out of sight the warrior took out his hunting knife and cut Graham's throat so quickly he had no time to scream. Quickly and skillfully he removed Graham's scalp and hung it from his belt smiling at the dead body that he left lying on the trail. In a matter of minutes he had trotted on and caught up with the others, leaving Graham's body for the vultures.

"What happened to Graham?" Captain Smith noticed that someone was missing, and began asking around when they stopped for the night. Everyone was resting after having eaten another supper of roasted deer and turkey, but they just shook their heads. When he looked at Tom there was a sadness that wasn't there the day before. "Tom? Do you know something I should know?"

"Master Graham ain't no more, sir." He was staring at one of the Indians as he spoke.

"What do you mean? Speak up, Tom." Captain Smith commanded.

Tom didn't move from the spot where he sat, leaning against a fallen log. "He dead, Captain. He dead. That there Indian done kilt him, and took his scalp."

Captain Smith turned and looked into the satisfied face of one of the warriors. The warrior grinned and patted the handle of his knife. Smith's face went white. Then he turned and paced the ground next to Peter.

"I have never felt so helpless. Here we are in the clutches of hostile Indians and helpless to do anything. They outnumber us. They have all the weapons."

Peter motioned for the Captain to sit down next to him and whispered, "Yes, Sir. I noticed the extra scalp hanging from that Indian's belt. He sure looks satisfied with his self."

"Yes. And that look just makes my blood boil." They both lowered their eyes when they saw the Indian glaring proudly.

When Cole realized what had happened to Graham he had no inclination to complain any further and tried hard to get along with the others. His legs were getting stronger and he was also losing weight and though he felt hungry most of the day he realized that Chief Gray Fox would probably kill him rather than put up with him.

"I reckon we all best get some rest." Peter spoke quietly. "I suspect tomorrow will be another climb up another mountain side. Up there at the top of that mountain," and he pointed toward the west, "we meet the divide. On the other side it should be mostly downhill. We be almost at the headwaters of these creeks."

"How do you know so much, Peter."

"Me and my brothers done a lot a huntin' in these parts. Wolf Creek became Clear Creek a ways back. It flows near where my brother Absalom discovered a new valley. We call it Abb's Valley.[3] He cleared some of the land and built a house. Other folks joined him.

"If you know this, then you know where they're taking us."

"Well, not exactly. I reckon we'll be going north o' the Ohio. I hear that's where most of the Shawnee live."

"Yes, I thought as much. I got as far as the Ohio last February on the Sandy River Expedition, but we didn't come this way. By the way, I knew of your brother, Robert, though I didn't know him personally. He was under William Preston's command."

"Yes, sir. I know. Captain Preston was kind enough to come by the house and talk to Bobby's wife, Margaret, and my ma. He left seven children. Benjamin is just a babe and Johnny is only ten." Peter picked up a twig and absent mindedly scratched through the leaves that littered the ground.

"I'm sorry." Smith looked at Peter and saw the sadness he seldom showed.

"Nothin to be sorry for. He joined the militia same as the rest of us. We do miss him."

"That whole expedition was a disaster from the beginning."

"How so?"

Smith took a deep breath as the memory returned. "We thought we were following a path least likely to attract the attention of the Indians. But, I guess you can't travel two hundred miles with three hundred forty men and even more horses without being spotted.

"It be certain they knew your plan when they spotted ya. You were probably seen by a huntin' party and they would a sent word to other parties. They scatter over the whole country south of the Ohio when they hunt in the winter. It be understood among the different tribes that that whole area is reserved for huntin' only. And you entered their huntin' territory. I'm surprised they let ya be. Maybe your greater number was in your favor; each huntin' party wouldn't be big enough to push you back. But, they would know where to hide as you passed by." Peter smiled slightly as he looked at Smith from the corner of his eye.

"I don't know, but we nearly starved to death. The Indians probably scared off the game so we wouldn't have anything to eat. Smith had been observing the three Frenchmen. "Think we'll see more French soldiers?"

"I don't know, but I wouldn't be surprised, especially north of the Ohio. If you'll pardon me, Sir, I'll bed down now." Peter moved away to a spot where he could be alone.

Captain John Smith was a born soldier. His father was a soldier and moving into the Blue Ridge Valley seemed like the best of both worlds. He had a farm of his own and only a few more years before he could retire to that farm. He had looked forward to being a gentleman farmer with ties to local politics. Now there was no one left on the farm but his wife and a young daughter. He dared not think how they would manage without him.

More days passed and Peter's boots had holes in the soles. Using a sharp stone he worked on pieces of bark, smoothing one side enough to stuff inside his boot with the smooth side toward his feet.

Before leaving the next morning Levisa put more charcoal into the pocket of her dress and Charlotte tore a small piece from her petticoat. She planned to save it for a moment when it seemed best to drop and mark the trail.

Chapter V

"Over here, Mr. Vause." Josh Miller shouted as he stood a good hundred yards ahead of the party waving his arm. "They left the creek here. It ain't gonna be hard to follow their trail now. Must be a hundred of 'em." Josh had been impatient to find something on his own and wanted to ingratiate himself to Ephraim Vause. He had always liked Levisa but was too shy to speak to her.

"Thanks, Josh." Vause looked at the prints. The side of the creek was torn up by horses' hooves, boots and moccasins. The red clay mud had been churned up while still wet making it difficult to pick out individual prints. This spot was easy to find. "They aren't even trying to cover their trail. I wonder if they want us to follow." The question both delighted and frightened him. "What if they lay a trap for us?"

Thirty-four men had combed both sides of the creek for three miles before finding the spot where the Indians and captives moved off. The column of men slowly followed the trail up the bank, leading them into the forest of leaves, twigs, bushes and briars.

"Best we follow on foot through this undergrowth. You men spread out on either side of me. Look for spore, broken branches, or overturned rocks. Damn. It would be easy to lose their trail in here. Damn Indians knew what they were doing comin this way.

"With so many on foot we'll catch 'em," exclaimed Jimmy Mann. Then under his breath he added, "I aim to show them savages a thing

26

or two." Jimmy lost his brother in March on Reed Creek, and had been only too happy to join the search party.

"Take it easy, Jimmy," cautioned Vause. "They're still a day ahead of us, and this dense wood makes it harder for us to follow. Ya gotta remember we're getting more and more into their territory. We have no idea what's ahead of us."

"Sure wish we had a really good tracker with us. We be farmers. I ain't never had to track anything before." Bobby Tracy mumbled.

"I tracked a bear once," offered Josh.

"Did you get it?" asked Bobby.

"Well. No. I lost him."

"Then you ain't no better'n the rest of us." Bobby might have found this funny under better circumstances but he, like the others was too worried about the safety of the captives.

Vause listened rather impatiently to their senseless chatter before speaking. "Gentlemen, I suggest you put your minds to looking for signs, anything that looks out of the ordinary."

They walked leading their horses up the same steep, rocky ravines the Indians had followed. Ephraim Vause grew exasperated, "Damn those Indians."

"I suspect we wouldn't be havin' so much trouble with the Indians if it weren't for the Frenchies buyin' 'em off like they been doin'. Hey, Mr. Vause. Look at this." Josh reached down and picked up something that had been partially covered by dirt.

"My god. It's a piece of blue ribbon." He turned it over in his hand reverently, certain it had to have come from a woman's dress. Could it belong to one of the women they were following?

Josh Miller stood staring at it. "It could be Miss Levisa's. She's kinda partial to blue. At least she always . . . ."

Josh blushed as Vause lifted one eyebrow and looked at the sandy haired young man. "Are you sweet on my Levisa, Josh?"

"Yes, sir. I . . I am. If'n you don't mind, Sir." Then he stood up and took a deep breath. "Now, I ain't said nothin' to her. I swear. I just kind a notice from afar."

Vause smiled at the young man in front of him, and then nodded his head. "It's okay, Josh. If we get her back I'll speak to her. But, first we gotta get her back."

"Yes, sir."

"That looks like rain clouds up ahead. That could wash out their tracks."

"But, if they continue up the New River, we can just follow the river like they do."

"And what if they leave the river? Timothy Motes, you and Johnny Pepper swim over to the other side and look for tracks. Better do it now before the river rises. I don't like the look of them clouds. The rest of us will look on this side. If they leave the river they'll probably follow a creek somewhere."

"Yes, sir." Timmy and Johnny gave their horses a little kick with their heels and went into the water.

"Hold onto the saddle, Timmy. Give him his head. He'll swim." Johnny yelled over the noise of the current.

"I'm holdin' on. This river be faster than it looked from shore," Timmy yelled back.

Johnny kept watching the water in front of him and didn't see the log coming down the middle of the river.

"Watch out fir that log, Johnny." Vause watched both men and horses as they struggled against the current. The log hit his horse in the rump and Johnny went into the river. "Johnny. Johnny. Grab the reins, grab somethin'." He saw Johnny's head go under and he kept yelling. "Johnny, where are you?" Johnny came up on the downriver side of his horse, barely grabbing the horse's mane before the current pulled him under again.

Timmy's horse managed to find bottom and started climbing out of the river on the other side. Johnny's horse was about ten yards behind. Timmy lay prone on the bank and turned to see Johnny hanging onto a tree limb. He crawled to the edge and reached out.

"Grab my hand, Johnny. I'll pull you out." Johnny worked his way along the branch until he was within reach. Once on the bank, both men collapsed.

On the other side of the river they heard shouting. "Timmy. They be callin. You answer 'em."

Timmy stood up and waved. Vause had ridden downriver to stand across from the two wet men. "Are you okay over there?"

"We be okay, Mr. Vause. Just wore out from fightin' the river current. The horses be okay too. We'll backtrack down river to look for signs."

"Give a yell if you see anything."

The main part of the group followed the trail as the rain began to fall. A few hours later the clouds opened up and the rescue party found themselves in a downpour. The rain continued for an hour and before long the river began to rise and become a raging torrent. The rain was accompanied by a strong wind that tore at their clothing, and successfully blew away a few hats. As the rained battered the leaves on their way to the ground the splattering noise increased.

They camped for the night along a ravine under large trees and a rock overhang. There was too little room for all of them, but it allowed them to build a fire. There was nothing to eat.

Johnny tried to dry his clothes. "This here fire give out more smoke than anything."

"I'd rather have dry clothes that smell like smoke than sleep in wet ones under a blanket that's wet," replied Timmy.

"At least you didn't fall in the river." Johnny pulled off his pants and shirt and hung them over some sticks near the fire. We ain't got anything to eat, do we?"

"I ain't. And you better check your musket and powder lest they be wet too. At least the rain stopped."

"Well, that's somethin'. Dang it all." His boots were sitting next to the fire and Johnny wrapped a wet blanket around his naked body as Timmy put a few more logs on the fire.

The next day Johnny and Timmy joined the rest of the party and followed the trail. It was getting easier to follow. Around mid morning they noticed vultures flying around in circles overhead.

"Mr. Vause, those vultures mean somthin's dead up ahead."

"Yes, Johnny, I know, and it makes me sick to think what it might be."

When they reached the spot and frightened away the vultures they found what was left of a horse. "It has to belong to one of the Indians. It's not shod and the harness is made of rope, definitely made by an Indian."

"Yeah! That ain't no white man's horse," exclaimed Josh." He held one hand over his nose and mouth to avoid the sickening smell of the dead animal that had begun to swell in the heat.

They left the carcass to the vultures and moved on.

Late that afternoon they found the body of a white man. "He's been scalped. Reckon we know who done this but who is it?" The men all shook their heads. The clothes were no different from their own, and without the scalp they were confused. "Well, he has to be one of those from the fort. It ain't Captain Smith. He would a wore his uniform." There weren't enough clues to his identity. "The vultures done tore up his face."

"I wonder who else they will murder before this is over?" Josh turned and ran behind a tree after looking at the decimated face that was beyond recognition.

"Let's hurry up and get him buried. We got a long ways to go yet." Vause spoke a few words over the grave, words he had learned from other burials he had attended. No one had thought to bring a bible.

Chapter VI

From the top of the divide Peter stopped to gaze through a break in the trees. One huge mountain range lay before him with inundating waves of deep green, to blue so pale it seemed to blend into the sky. The sun was at its peak with only a few puffs of clouds; a pure, clean unspoiled land. An eagle flew nearby calling to its mate, or just calling for the sheer joy of free flight. Peter couldn't pause for long. The warrior behind poked him with the barrel of his musket, and Peter walked on with one eye on the scenery. The peacefulness of the landscape reminded him of the hunting trips he took with his brothers and the days they would sit and breathe in the beauty of the wilderness. *Oh, to enjoy days like that again.* His heart ached to be with his brothers on a trip through the wilderness. They were some of the happiest days of his young life.

On the western side of the divide they followed a small ravine downhill into the forest. That evening they camped near a small pool that had formed next to several large boulders. The horses had plenty of room to graze, and several of the captives laid down in exhaustion in a small meadow of soft grass.

"Jessica. I want to go swimming." Sarah begged.

"Oh, go on. What do I care? But keep your dress on or I'll whip you good." Jessica looked longingly at the clear still water. She too wanted to swim but worried about how she would look if she got wet all over. Maybe she would walk into the water to cool off.

"That's a good idea." Charlotte followed Sarah into the water and began to rub the dirt from her clothes. "Come on Levisa. It will feel good to be clean again." Within minutes all the girls and women were in the water helping each other to bathe with their clothes on.

"I feel like I haven't had a bath in a coon's age, remarked Mary Ingles. "If only we had some soap we could wash our hair."

"Lean over and I'll help you do your hair," Mrs. Vause said as she approached Mary. "Charlotte, you and Levisa help each other. Sarah, come here and I'll help you."

"I want to swim first." Sarah dogpaddled back and forth in the shallow parts of the stream, laughing as if she hadn't a care in the world.

After her swim Sally Henderson disappeared into the woods. The water made her long skirts heavy and she wanted to wring out the dress but needed complete privacy. No one paid any attention when she left but Christopher Hicks followed her. Sally found a mossy spot surrounded by large oak trees and pulled off her clothes to ring out the water. Christopher threw his arms around her and held her tight. "Don't scream. It's only me, Chris. I promise I won't hurt you." He whispered into one ear.

"And just what do you think you're about, Mr. Hicks? Let me go."

"I love ya, Sally. I love ya something awful." He continued to hold onto her naked body, and began to run his hands along her breasts and hips.

"Awful is right. Now let me go or I'll scream."

"No." He put one hand over her mouth and nearly cut off her breathing. "Sally, nobody's gonna find us. We be given to the Indians. They'll make a squaw out of ya. But, I'm gonna have ya before they do."

She struggled and tried to scream through his tight grip over her mouth. He pushed her onto the ground. She beat him with her fists, but he held her tight and without much trouble he was on top of her. When he was done he stood up and looked down at her.

"You be mine now, Sally. My woman. Nobody elses." He left her lying on the ground crying uncontrollably.

Sally dressed in her wet clothes and returned to the river. She walked a few yards away from the others and stood in waist deep water. She then began to walk into deeper water, but it was never deep enough so she sat down bringing the water over her head. Her hair floated on the surface as bubbles emerged.

Tom had walked along the river after taking a swim and saw the blonde hair and bubbles. He dove into the river and within two strokes reached her and pulled her up. She coughed instinctively and sputtered. She noticed his strong, black arm around her waist and began to cry. "Just leave me, Tom. I want to die right here and right now."

"Why fore you want to go and do a thing like that?"

"I just do. You wouldn't understand. I just do. Please." Her begging was weak and she didn't fight. Instead she let him pull her from the river and put her down on a fallen tree and sat beside her and let her cry. She ignored her water logged clothing and buried her face in her hands.

Tom continued to sit, watching over her. No one else paid any attention to her. Most had already returned to the camp and didn't notice that she and Tom were missing. It took awhile for her to compose herself. When she was ready Tom walked with her back to the camp.

Captain Smith sat down next to Peter who had leaned against a tree with his legs stretched out in front of him. "Peter, have you ever been here before?"

"No, Sir. We never crossed the divide. We did all our huntin' on the other side. But, I wouldn't mind comin' back to this place." The forced march hadn't bothered Peter, except for the hostile looks from the warriors. "My only problem right now is what to do when these boots wear out completely. I put bark in the bottom, but before long the holes be too big to hold the bark."

The poultice applied by Chief Gray Fox had been a big help in healing the wounds suffered by Peter and the two Robinson brothers. So far, there had been no ill health among any of the captives. Even Mr. Cole had quit his whining after the death of Mr. Graham. That alone could be a reason to rejoice.

Sarah amused herself by talking to anyone who would listen, and one evening she found herself standing in front of Chief Gray Fox. Her hair had been combed with a smooth twig and braded by Charlotte. It was tied with a piece of cloth from Charlotte's skirt. After a swim in the creek Sarah was looking about as good as possible under trying circumstances. The swim had even cleaned up her dress. "Little girl not cry any more. Gray Fox glad to see little girl in good spirit."

"I guess I'm okay. I have my sister and father for company."

"Which one father?"

Sarah pointed to Ivan Medley who was sitting next to Jessica as she tried to put some order to her own hair. "Father to you and that girl?"

"Yes, I'm Sarah and that's my sister, Jessica. My father is Ivan Medley."

"How come you not have red hair like sister?"

"My mother had red hair. Mine is like my father's."

"Where mother?"

"She died of fever last winter."

Sarah stood tall and looked straight into Chief Gray Fox's eyes as she spoke. She had grown less and less afraid of him in these past two weeks. When he spoke to her his eyes had a gentleness about them but in an instant his expression was hard and he turned and walked away.

The further west they went the easier the streams were to cross. Those on foot were able to wade, stumbling a little on slippery, lichen covered rocks that lay submerged and hidden from view. Levisa continued to write her name on sycamore and beech trees.

"If only we could have something besides deer, turkey and fish to eat. I'm sick and tired of the same old thing. And I'm sick and tired of sitting on a horse day after day. My backside is sore." She sulked a bit as she chewed the meat that was burnt on the outside and mostly raw inside. "What I wouldn't give for a piece of cornbread with a hunk of butter."

Levisa and Charlotte had given up counting all the creeks they crossed. "I've been counting the days, and I reckon it's the middle of July."

"Oh, Levisa. I wish I had thought to do that," spoke Mrs. Vause. "I suppose that's something to keep your mind on."

"Yes, mother. I know you worry about us, but you needn't. Charlotte and I will be just fine."

"Bless you, Levisa. You always were one to keep a clear head. I just pray your father finds us soon."

Mary Engels sat down next to Mrs. Vause. "You have two wonderful girls, Mrs. Vause. You must be very proud of them. Now, little Sarah Medley is probably the best ambassador of good will of anyone in the camp. I envy her innocence and good spirit. Bless her heart. Because of my sister-in-law's experience last year, I'm certain they will be treated well as Shawnee women, and according to her they won't be forced into marriage. But, before any of this happened I told my John I wanted to go east to avoid this very problem we're facing, but he didn't want to go so far away from our farm. Now, he's dead and I'm in the hands of the very Indians I hoped I would never see. What good is that farm to me now? Without my John I'd just as soon they put an end to my suffering."

Mrs. Vause put a comforting arm around Mary's shoulders. "I pray every night that Ephraim has a scouting party out looking for us." She looked at her servant girl, Sally, who was sitting alone. "I wonder what's going on in that head of hers. She hasn't said a word to me since we began this journey."

"I suspect she sees it as a way out of bondage."

"A way out? She only has four more years and her debt to us for her passage to America will be paid in full. She would be free to go wherever she wants. She'll get a whole barrel of corn, an ox or horse and fifty acres of land for herself. I've seen no prospects of marriage, but I'm sure someone would come along between now and then. She's not hard to look at, though that blonde hair makes her look a little washed out. Peter Looney seems like a likely one, and he comes from a good family. They have plenty of property, and I understand they had just acquired more. In fact he has two-hundred-fifty acres in his own name and him not more than twenty-two years of age."

"Why would Peter want to marry a serving girl? With his family's influence he would want better."

"There's nothing wrong with Sally. She just needs to know her place. She gets a little uppity at times."

Sally Henderson noticed Mrs. Vause looking at her and was glad she didn't have to do her bidding anymore. It was almost worth being a captive to be out of the way of that woman and her whipping stick. The woman thought too much of herself. Then she noticed Christopher Hicks watching her. The look in his eyes made her nervous and she was glad to have Tom sitting beside her.

Sally looked at Sarah and smiled. "So young and so innocent. Even the Indians show a fondness for her, if fondness is what you could call their usually cold faces. But, I've seen Chief Gray Fox smile sometimes when he thought none of us was watchin'."

Tom looked at Sally's sad face and wondered why she had tried to drown herself. "Who you talkin to, Sally?" She didn't look at him, and seemed to be talking to herself.

Sally looked up with a start, "Sorry, Tom." She noticed his bare feet. "How are your feet?"

"They don't bother me none. My feet be about as tough as any hide I ever seed."

Are you gettin' enough to eat?"

"Shore. They don't treat me no different from you white folks."

"Well, that's somethin, ain't it?"

Chapter VII

Christopher Hicks followed Sally to the river, but before she had gone past two large trees and a few bushes he grabbed her and dragged her into the woods. A warrior noticed Hicks follow Sally, and out of curiosity he followed Hicks. When Hicks threw Sally to the ground the warrior grabbed him and cut his throat. Sally screamed.

Most of the camp was in the woods as soon as they heard the scream.

Sarah looked toward the sound and jumped, "what was that?"

"Maybe somebody got caught by a bear," exclaimed Jessica. She had seen Hicks follow Sally but didn't think anything of it.

When Chief Gray Fox saw the dead man on the ground he asked why. The warrior did not speak English, but he answered in Shawnee. "Man do dishonor to woman."

Sally got up and ran back to the camp crying hysterically. Captain Smith ran behind her. "Sally. What happened? Why would that Indian kill Hicks? He was such a quiet man."

"He may be quiet but he was no gentleman. He grabbed me and pushed me onto the ground. That Indian saved me."

"The Indian saved you? I had no idea they ever did such a thing."

"I didn't either, but it's true."

When Gray Fox returned to the camp Captain Smith approached

him. "Chief. Sally told me that your warrior saved her from that man's attack. Is that true?"

"Woman speak true. Him bad man."

"Well. I don't quite know what to say, but I'm very glad to hear of it. Thank you."

Later, everyone noticed the additional scalp hanging from the belt of the warrior who had killed Hicks.

"Chief?" Captain Smith spoke again. "We should bury Hick's body. Would you allow us to do that? Even though he disgraced himself he still deserves a Christian burial."

"We not wait for that. We leave now." Chief Gray Fox scowled and turned away.

Captain Smith went back to Sally and put an arm around her shoulder. "You don't get much respect or attention from our little party, do you?"

"That's to be expected. I'm only a servant. I reckon that's one step up from being a slave, and slaves don't get any attention at all. I'll be okay now, Captain. Thank you." As Sally spoke she continued to shake uncontrollably. Mary approached and held her close until the shaking stopped. Then they were called to move out.

When they stopped that evening the entire camp hummed with whispers. Ivan Medley was possibly the only one not whispering rumors and accusations.

"I can't sleep, Daddy, tell me a story." Sarah curled up as close to her father as possible, but he didn't move a muscle. "Daddy? Why won't you talk to me anymore? You used to before we was captured. Daddy?"

"Sarah, leave him alone. Can't you see he doesn't want to be bothered." Jessica pulled at her little arms. "Come over here and sit by me. I'll tell you a story."

"But, why can't daddy tell me a story?"

"Because he can't. Now stop asking questions. Come and lay your head on my lap. I'll tell you the story about baby Jesus and you can go to sleep." Jessica stroked Sarah's hair as she began the story. She caught a glimpse of Gray Fox and was surprised to realize he seemed to be listening as he sharpened his knife.

Ivan Medley had not moved from where he sat. The one love in his life was his wife and she died the winter before of a fever. There was no doctor to call, and Jessica knew nothing about medicine. He was unable to save her. Now, he saw her almost nightly in his dreams and if he had one wish it would be to join her.

They were so far into Indian country that the captives were being given a little more freedom. None had tried to run away because they knew it would be useless. The Indians and French soldiers had all the weapons. They also controlled the horses.

William Pepper was leaning against a tree chewing on a twig. He had been watching Jessica, ever since their capture. To him she was the unattainable dream and thought she was more beautiful than any girl he had ever known.

Jimmy Bell, another young man looked at William. "Billy Boy, why don't ya go talk to her. You like her don't ya?"

"She don't even know I exist." He continued to watch as she told Sarah a story.

Jimmy Bell had also been watching Jessica. He knew she was pretty, but he also knew she liked to flirt. He'd been around her a few times at dances and noticed the way she batted those green eyes at young men, though never at him.

Jimmy followed Jessica when she walked to the river. When she knelt down to get a drink of water he put one hand over her mouth, and an arm around her waist. He pulled her into the bushes. She kicked and tried to hit him, but Jimmy was stronger and a lot taller.

William Pepper also saw Jessica leave. He also saw Jimmy follow her. William followed both of them but was confused when he didn't see either of them at the creek. He looked around. Bushes were being shaken by something, and he heard a groan. It was not an animal sound, but definitely human. He went to check.

What he saw made his blood boil. "Leave her alone, Jimmy." Her skirts had been pulled up to her waist. He threw one arm around Jimmy's neck and pulled him back. "Run, Jessica. Run." He threw Jimmy to the ground and then hit him. One blow to his chin and another to his eye. Jessica jumped up and ran as quickly as she could. The two men continued hitting each other then rolling on the ground with first one on top and then the other, slinging their fists until blood began to flow. Jimmy fell to the ground, but William pulled him up by his hair and hit him again. Blood flew from Jimmy's cut lip.

Jessica ran back to the camp and told Chief Gray Fox that the two were fighting.

"Why they fight?" He stared at her and guessed the answer from the terrified look in her eyes.

Jessica just stared at him. She couldn't find the words to make him understand. So she lied, "I don't know. They just are."

"Maybe one kill the other. Then we have one less to feed." Gray Fox did not feel like being bothered.

However, Captain Babbee laughed and decided to go watch the fun. The rest of the captives overheard and ran to watch the fight. Both men were giving the other a pretty good beating by the time others showed up.

"Okay, stop it, both of you," commanded Captain Smith. "Get down to the creek and wash the blood off, then go back to the camp. I want none of this fighting among ourselves.

"But, Captain." William started to explain and then decided against it. He didn't want to mention Jessica's name. When the Captain gave him a push he went to the creek and threw water on his face. He pulled his shirt off and rinsed the blood in the water. Jimmy did the same. They stood several yards away from each other and whenever their eyes met, they glared with uncontrolled hatred.

Jessica approached William when he returned to the camp, "Thank you, William. You were very brave."

"Don't mention it." He looked hard into her eyes. "I mean it. Don't mention it to anybody."

She shook her head. "I understand. Maybe you could escort me the next time I go for a drink of water. I'd be grateful."

"Sure." He watched her walk away. *Well, I reckon she knows who I am now. That's something.*

If Jessica wasn't sitting with the women she sat next to William. His shyness actually made her feel safe. She knew he wouldn't hurt her. "Jessica, do you mind if I ask you a question about your Pa?"

"I reckon so. What is it?" They were resting against the same large oak tree and waiting for the food to be roasted over the fire.

"He don't seem quite right. Is he sick?"

"No, he ain't sick unless you mean in the head. He ain't been the same since our Ma died last winter. It's okay with me if he never talks to me again. After Ma died he thought I should be just like her, cook and keep house and look after Sarah like nothing ever happened."

"I'm sorry. It must have been hard on you." He was sympathetic but thought that was what all women did anyway and wondered by she would complain about it.

"Yes, it was, and not a kind word from him."

On another occasion William was sitting against a tree. He had always been thin but after three weeks on the trail he was even more so. The only item that didn't hang on him was the tri-cornered hat he always wore.

Sarah bounded over to William and sat down next to him with her head tilted one way and then another, as if he was a strange puzzle she had to figure out. "What ya doin', William?"

"Nothin'. I ain't doin' nothin'. Go bother somebody else, why don't ya."

"Where did you get that hat you wear all the time?"

"It used to belong to my Pa. My Ma give it to me just days before I went to the fort to help defend it."

"Is your Pa dead?"

"Yes, and you shouldn't ask such questions."

"I'm sorry. You like Jessica, don't ya?"

"It's none of your business. She just ask me to escort her to the creek so nobody will bother her. I could do the same for you if you want. And if you be good."

"Naa. I don't need no escortin'. But, maybe Jessica does."

"Go away." William's face turned bright red and he stood up and walked away.

For a six year old Sarah was handling the journey well. Time was today. She didn't dwell on yesterdays, and tomorrow was tomorrow. She took each day as it came, and since everyone including Chief Gray Fox was good to her, she had nothing to fear. She knew that Hicks was killed for doing something bad, and no one mentioned Graham to her. She didn't know the man and was barely aware of his absence. The only family she had was with her. Mary Engels and Mrs. Vause often told her stories or sang to her. She didn't mind sitting horseback every day, and since the horse only walked it was quite comfortable. She swayed back and forth as the horse walked and sometimes she even dozed in her sister's arms.

Mary Ingles and Mrs. Vause frequently sat together. They tried to keep their conversations on the scenery, or some light topic, but tonight Mary couldn't hold back her misery and hatred for the Indians. "I don't know how I'll go on without John."

"I know you're hurting, Mary, but you've got to hold up. Don't allow them to know how much you hurt. Be proud. The Indians will think better of you for it. Look at how the Chief looks at Sarah. If he didn't look so frightening I'd swear he almost smiles at times, especially at Sarah, if you can call that a smile."

"I'm pretty sure he likes her, but what will that mean when they get us to where they're taking us?" Out of mutual fear, the topic of what would become of them when they reached the Indian village was one they avoided.

"Captain Smith thinks they will take us to one of their towns across the Ohio River."

"That's so far. I wonder how much longer till we get there, do you think?" Mary was sitting cross legged and pulled the remnants of her skirt over her ankles. Then, with a forked twig she began to pull at the knots in her hair. There were no ribbons to tie it, so her hair hung down her back in long brown waves.

"Captain Smith says it may be several more days before we reach the Ohio. He was there in February, but they ran into a lot of trouble. The militia he was with ran out of food and nearly starved but for some bits of buffalo they found drying along a river. They chewed that to keep alive."

"He was here?"

"No, not this river. He said they were on another river that we crossed a few days ago."

"I'll be glad to see an end to this traveling whatever happens."

Chapter VIII

Gunfire exploded. The Indians fired their muskets into the air, and the sudden sharp noise was so frightening to some of the men that three of them fell to the ground. When they realized they had not been shot they got back on their feet and looked at each other sheepishly as they dusted off their pants. The other captives looked confused. Captain Babbee and Chief Gray Fox turned and laughed. The Indians raised their rifles into the air and began whooping and yelling.

"Why are they yelling?" asked Levisa. "I don't see anything."

Peter stood beside Levisa's horse. "Must be the Ohio," Peter remarked as he looked at the river. "It be wider than any I ever did see in me whole life. Maybe they just be happy to be here."

"Do you think we're close to their town? Could that be why they seem so happy?" Levisa asked. The Indians hollered for several minutes before stopping.

"I reckon it can't be too far yet."

Sarah looked confused. "I don't see any town. Where's it at?"

"It must be on the other side of the river," Jessica answered.

"But, I don't see any ferry, and I can't swim. How will we get across? Jessica, you have to help me." As they drew closer to the river it seemed even larger.

"Oh, hush up, Sarah. Don't be such a crybaby."

"I'm not cryin', I was just askin', that's all." Sarah wiped away a tear.

Jessica dismounted and pulled Sarah off the horse.

Peter took Sarah by the hand and walked with her to the river's edge. "Don't worry, Sarah. You've been a brave girl. The Indians have a plan. I'm certain."

Chief Gray Fox held up his hand. "This not place to cross. Get back on horse."

"Okay, Sarah. Up you go." Peter lifted Sarah back onto the horse.

They moved east from the confluence of the Ohio to another river that flowed in from the north. Then Chief Grey Fox dismounted.

Peter helped Sarah dismount and she held onto his hand, "Peter, will you help me? I'm scared. I can't swim that far. If they make me swim I'll drown. Please."

"Hey, so all of a sudden I'm Peter and no more Mr. Looney." Peter picked her up and hugged her. "Well I don't think you'll even get your big toe wet." He pinched one of her toes and she giggled. "That's better now. And would you look there? Canoes. Six of 'em." He put Sarah back on the ground and she watched as the canoes were pulled up along the shore.

"We all can't fit into those," complained Jessica. Peter turned away from her and walked over to a large sycamore tree that leaned precariously over the water. He leaned against the tree to rest a moment.

With his back to Levisa he whispered, "You're gettin' mighty good at this," She discreetly wrote her name with a piece of charcoal she had pulled from her pocket. Peter looked at her dress. Her pocket was black with smudge, but when she straightened her apron it was carefully covered.

"Hush! This could be my last chance. We don't know what's on the other side of that river."

"We didn't know what we would see on this side. What's the difference?"

"Now that we've finally reached the Ohio I'm starting to worry about what will happen to us on the other side.

"Is this the first you've felt afraid?"

"Yes and no. I was horribly frightened when they first captured us, but after several days I realized they weren't going to hurt us. Now, I feel that crossing that river will mean great changes. I was almost hoping we would never get to their village. Once in that village we don't know what to expect. I kept praying that my father would find us before now."

Peter put a hand on her shoulder. "Levisa. You mustn't fret so. You're young, healthy and very smart. They may treat you very well."

"Peter. You don't know that."

"I used to hear the Cherokee speak of such matters. I do believe you will be treated well."

Captain Babbee grabbed one of the captives by the shoulder and pointed to the canoes. "Get in." Then he did the same with five more until there was one prisoner and five Indians in each canoe. The rest of the captives watched as the canoes were paddled across, each one paddling hard against the flow of the river. The horses were lead into the water. Each one with its head held high and neighing, reluctant to enter such a wide river.

When it was Sarah's turn she held onto Jessica's hand. "Please let me go with my sister."

Chief Gray Fox heard her plea. "Little girl go with sister."

Once everyone had crossed they remounted the horses.

"I thought we were near their town. Where on earth is it? They all whooped and hollered like they could see it." Jessica complained. "This horse is wet."

Peter had been walking beside Jessica, but he was tired of her whining and moved ahead to walk beside Levisa and Charlotte who continued to share the same horse. The crossing had taken a few hours and now it was late afternoon.

Peter lifted his head and sniffed the air. "Smoke. I smell smoke."

"Yes. So do I," replied Captain Smith."

"Look, I see smoke." Someone ahead called. The further they walked the hazier the air became.

"It's got to be their town. You'll be able to stop soon, Levisa." Peter looked up at her and her eyes were wide and her jaws were clinched tight. Her lips had turned white. Charlotte also looked frightened. He patted them each on their bare ankles.

The afternoon quiet was broken by the sound of dogs barking. The braves began whooping and yelling again, but this time the yelling was returned from others up ahead. Several young Indians approached on ponies. A bend in the river gave the captives their first glimpse of an Indian town. It covered a broad expanse along both sides of the river. Men, women and children came out of their homes and gathered in groups to watch as the party of captives passed by. Some of the warriors broke away and greeted their families. Children ran back and forth poking and taunting the captives. As the children struck at the feet of the girls Jessica yelled back at them, but that only made the children laugh.

Over three hundred wigwams made up the Shawnee town. The captives and the warriors walked or rode into the center stopping in the large clearing. On one side was a very long building, about ninety feet long, large enough to hold most of the adult residents.

The captives dismounted and their horses were taken away. As they stood still the warriors tied their hands behind them then pushed them toward two poles stuck in the ground.

"You stay," announced the chief, then turned and walked away as the captives were tied to the poles. They all sat down on the ground and waited. No one came to give them water. No one paid any attention. Ebenezer Cole finally broke his silence.

"They'll burn us at the stake for sure. I knew it would happen, but none of you would believe me. Now, you'll see I was right. I was right all along."

"Cole. For the love of God, shut up," Captain Smith demanded.

"Why should I? I told you this would happen, and you sneered at me."

"For the last time, Cole, shut your mouth or I'll suggest you be the first to die."

Cole stopped talking, but shivered at the thought of dying.

There they remained on the ground, in the blazing sun. Finally a little water was given to each one, but the smell of food cooking over open fires throughout the village filled the air.

"Can't you smell that food? Why won't they feed us?" Jessica complained.

"My mouth is watering like never before." Mary Englis asserted.

"Those seasonings smell so good. It seems like forever since we had beans and squash. It's almost too much to bear." Charlotte admitted.

"I do believe I will expire if I don't have something to eat soon. I can smell those beans. If only I could have some now," Jessica whined.

"Shut up, Jessica." Levisa barked. "If my hands weren't tied I'd smack you senseless. I'm sick of your whining. You have no rights and it's time you faced it. Just pray they feed us today."

"You're just jealous. You've always been jealous because the boys liked me better, and I know Captain Babbee likes me. I could tell by the way he looked at me. I think he was just waiting until we got here before he released me."

"Oh, bosh." Levisa gave Jessica a kick with her foot and twisted around so she wouldn't have to look at her.

"Owe! You have no call to kick me." Jessica pulled her legs up close to her chest.

Cole muttered to himself, lowly and inaudibly to the others. Captain Smith was not close enough to poke him, but William Robinson was and he poked him with his elbow. "The Captain told you to shut up."

The captives were ignored as they sat for what seemed like an intolerable length of time. "A little water and we wait until they finish their supper." Jessica could not stop. "I wonder where Captain Babbee went? He'll come and untie me. I'm sure of it."

Mrs. Vause looked at Jessica's dirty face sympathetically and shook her head. "I suspect they have a welcoming ceremony planned, but we have arrived at an inconvenient moment for them." She had overheard Captain Smith talk, but didn't care to speak of it. They would find out soon enough for themselves.

After a while the smell of food was gone and with it any hope the captives had of being fed.

Women and children began to congregate in the center of the village carrying sticks and pine branches. They commented among themselves as they looked over these white people. The children poked them with sticks, and their mothers laughed as they pulled them away. Then those same women and children were joined by others until the captives were surrounded. They all moved toward the lodge as they chatted, and formed two long lines that led to the lodge. Their chatter was melodious but none of the captives could understand any of it.

The lodge was built much like the wigwams, but with taller saplings, bent to form the latticed structure and covered with the bark of many trees. It was by far the largest structure in the village.

Some of the children played with sticks while they waited for the ceremony to begin. They lunged and parried as fencers would.

The village chief approached Captain John Smith and untied him. Once Smith was on his feet and about twenty paces away from the others, two older squaws pulled off his boots, his stockings, shirt and finally his pants leaving him completely naked. His white flesh and light brown hair was in stark contrast to the brown skins and black hair of the Shawnee. The same two squaws led him to the front of the line; the front being farthest from the lodge. He stared into the wicked and snarling faces of the women and children, some hardly big enough to lift the branch they held, and they looked back at Captain Smith with grim faces. Some of the elders showed toothless grinning mouths as they chuckled with savage glee.

"Some welcoming committee you are, you heathen savages." Smith muttered under his breath. Then he stood tall and as he waited he prayed, "Dear Lord, do not let me fail this test. See me through to the end and help me to bare the cuts and bruises with dignity."

"You run. You fall down, you start over. You run to lodge." Captain Smith only glared at the chief. The chief hit him on the back with a stick every bit as big as those held by some of the women. That hit momentarily took the wind from his lungs, but he quickly inhaled and started running. The sticks and branches cut across his legs, arms and torso. He tried to focus on the lodge, but as some of the branches came up higher he held up an arm to shield his face and eyes from the hits that left welts and blood in stripes across his body.

Smith bit his lip to control the pain, and stumbled when a squaw hit him hard on the shin with a stick that was more a club than a stick. His hands touched the ground, but he didn't fall. The blows doubled in the few seconds he stumbled. An old woman whacked him across his back. In anger he screamed curses at them and continued on. When he at last touched the lodge he fell to his knees, breathing heavily.

Two young women escorted him into a nearby wigwam where they washed his wounds with clear, cool water and applied a poultice to them. When they finished nursing him, two other women brought him water and food, and left him alone to rest on a bed that was more like a bench hugging the walls of the wigwam. He lay exhausted on a buffalo robe. Inside the wigwam Smith looked around. The bench on which he lay ran around the entire circumference of the wigwam. The floor was covered with many woven mats and in the center was a ring of stones circling a fire pit. At the top of the roof was a square opening where light penetrated the dark interior. There was no fire in the middle of summer, and the only other light coming in was from the opening in the doorway. The buffalo flap over the door was pulled aside and fastened to stay open.

One by one the other men were stripped and forced to run the gauntlet, all managing to do so without too much trouble. One fell onto the ground and had to start over, doing so with a renewed determination. Ebenezer Cole cried and begged as he was dragged to the head of the line screaming to be let free. He stood naked as the others had at the front of the line, but when he looked at the angry faces of the women he dropped to the ground and curled up, crying.

"Take this one away. I want no more of this crying like little baby. Tie him to tall pole." The chief turned his back to Cole who whimpered in relief.

As he stood with his hands tied behind him and his back against the pole, he was faced toward the gauntlet. With a band around his forehead that tied his head to the pole, he could not turn away. He was forced to watch as each person ran the gauntlet among the laughter and cursing of the women.

Ivan Medley stood before the Shawnee women and children. His shoulders were slumped in submission. He walked as the blows landed and the clubs tore at his skin. Beyond caring, he began to stumble, and when he fell he was dragged back to the beginning. He stumbled again as soon as he began to walk. He fell again, and again he was pulled back to the beginning. The third time he was pushed into the gauntlet where he was surrounded by women and children who continued to beat him until he was unconscious. He was carried away and tied to a pole next to Ebenezer Cole.

Peter was the last of the men to run. It had taken a long time for all eleven of the men to run or be carried away. He wanted to get it over with. From watching the comings and goings at the wigwam he knew food and water would be his reward, and he was more thirsty than hungry. While sitting and watching each of the other men run and suffer the blows inflicted, his mouth felt as if someone had stuffed it with cotton. He was not afraid. If the other men could endure it so could he. He held his head up as the old women removed his clothing and stood in his bare feet as they removed his pants and what was left of his shirt. He ran his tongue over the roof of his mouth to bring up some saliva, but with little success. When he was taken to the front of the line he looked at the fierce expressions on the women, especially the older ones. He bowed and smiled. "Howdy do, ladies." They did not smile back. Instead they growled menacingly and the children laughed at him. They hurled words he couldn't understand.

"Cursing me are ya? Well, I'll show ya bloody savages. He took a deep breath as he waited for the blow to his shoulders. When it came he ran with all the determination he possessed. The Shawnee women and children had not tired one bit, and the older women especially seemed to gain strength from each runner. Peter watched the clubs knowing they could trip him. He jumped and ran stumbling briefly, but only once and he barely slowed down. He reached the lodge and leaned against it breathing heavily but refusing to give in to the pain. He stood and waited for the two young women to lead him away. Each cut on his back, chest, legs and arms was carefully and gently cleaned with fresh water and a poultice applied. His back and legs were decorated with bands running horizontally in a zigzagged pattern.

Then it was the women's turn. Mrs. Vause came first. She stood straight and held her head high as the old women untied the laces of her bodice, removed her apron, and then her petticoats, bodice and chemise. She stood with her clothing in a heap by her feet. She was glad the white men were inside the wigwam and could not see her. She glanced back at her two daughters whose heads were lowered in shame for their mother. Two Shawnee women walked over and pulled back their heads and held them. There was horror in their eyes as tears blurred their vision and ran down their cheeks. Jessica stared straight ahead looking past Mrs. Vause. All color was drained from her face.

Sarah wanted to scream, but didn't dare. The Shawnee women standing nearby frightened her to the point of muteness. She had watched the men run and was ashamed for her father, but watching the women seemed even more horrible. She pressed close to Charlotte, the one sitting closest to her.

Mrs. Vause vowed to herself she would not be disgraced by failing this test of will and endurance. She stood at the front of the line and looked at the women and children before her as if to dare them to stop her from running the full length. She was slapped across the shoulder blades and in that instant began to run as fast as she could. She endured their blows and bit her lip to keep from crying out when the sticks and branches stung her arms, legs, and back. With welts forming across her breasts she could not hold back for long. When, at last she could stop at the lodge she fell to her knees, and she too was led away to a different wigwam. She was nursed just as the men were and given food, water and rest.

Levisa was the eldest of the four girls, and after Sally and Mary Engels ran, she was the next one to be stripped. Her embarrassment was almost more than she could bear. She bore it bravely until her chemise fell to the ground leaving her stark naked. She tried not to show it, but as she was led to the beginning of the line she tried to cover herself with her arms and hands. The Shawnee women and children laughed outrageously. Once slapped across her back she ran only to stumble. Half blinded by tears she got up and continued rather than let herself fall to the ground. With her hand on the lodge at last she crouched and cried loudly, "Oh, dear God in heaven, please help me." She too was led away.

Inside the wigwam her mother looked at her. "Oh, dear Levisa. I'm so sorry this had to happen to you."

"It's over now, mother. I'm sure I'll be okay in a few days." She lay down on the bench nearest her mother and waited as the two young women washed and nursed her. When the food and water arrived, she looked into faces of girls no older than herself. "Thank you," she said as softly as she could. One of them smiled briefly and they left.

Jessica waited; knowing she would be the next, and vowed she would not let her humiliation overtake her. She swore not to cry, but when her clothes were removed and the Indian women saw that her pubic hair was the same as the red hair on her head they all pointed and jabbered something she could not understand. She held up her head and shed no tears.

"I'm not afraid of you heathens," she said as she glared at them. However, fear replaced her brave words and it showed in her eyes. She was afraid of pain and she didn't know how she could avoid it. She looked around, thinking that Captain Babbee would put a stop to her torture, but he stood next to one of the wigwams and watched placidly with his arms folded across the front of his uniform. All belief of his being interested in her died. She realized her foolishness and as she braced herself for the signal to start her sight was blurred by the tears that formed. When slapped on the back she dug her bare feet into the dirt and ran. When she finally reached the lodge she knelt down with her back to the line of women and both hands on the bark of the lodge and cried. In that moment she became a little girl crying for her mother.

Charlotte and Sarah were deemed too young for the race and were therefore spared though they had sat and watched as each person ran and suffered. They were taken to the wigwam where the other female captives were kept, and at last they too were given food and water.

Charlotte looked around the dark interior. "I feel so sorry that you should suffer so."

Mary Ingles replied, "Don't worry, Charlotte. I have hope that the worse is over. We've all prayed that it is."

As evening came the village grew quiet but only for a short time. Sarah heard shouting and the voices of many people walking past the wigwam. She had always been a curious child and crept through the opening to see what was going on.

Not able to see through the mass of people gathered at the far end of the clearing, she quietly went around them and followed, keeping out of the way in case someone should change their mind about making her run the gauntlet. She saw the top of the poles where they had tied Mr. Cole and her father. When she got close enough she noticed they were piling wood all around the feet of the two men. She started to scream, but just as she opened her mouth Charlotte suddenly appeared and clamped a hand over it. She wrapped her other arm around the little girl and tried to lift her. Sarah was small but strong and she wiggled out of Charlotte's arms and ran toward her father.

"Daddy. Daddy." Her screams were heard over the voices of the people and they turned to stare and laugh at her. Chief Gray Fox heard her calling and pushed his way through the throng of people and grabbed her by the arm. He stared at her.

"You brave girl no more. Chief Gray Fox not happy with little girl." He dragged her over to where Charlotte stood. "You go back to wigwam. No make noise," he demanded.

Charlotte picked her up again and carried her in her arms. "Come, Sarah. Don't look back." Sarah cried great convulsive sobs, but she stopped struggling. "I'll sing you a song."

Sarah buried her face in Charlotte's chest and covered her ears so as not to hear any more. Charlotte sang loudly enough for all the women to hear and to cover the sound of Cole's screams. The other women joined Charlotte in singing hymns.

'The Lord is my Shepherd, no want shall I know;
I feed in green pastures, safe folded I rest; He leadeth
my soul where the still waters flow, Restores me when
wand'ring, redeems when oppressed; Restores me when
wand'ring, redeems when oppressed.'[4]

Ivan Medley stood next to Cole, and looked over the heads of the villagers. Both men stood stark naked and in their bare feet. Ivan Medley looked up at the sky and spoke one word, "Amy."

Mr. Cole's screams could be heard throughout the entire village as he begged and pleaded for his life. The Shawnee looked on and jeered angrily at him. They used burning sticks to poke at his naked body, and he screamed with each touch.

Ivan Medley closed his eyes, but could not close his ears to Cole's screaming. As the flames grew hotter he began to pray, "The Lord is my Sheppard; I shall not want. He maketh me to lie down in green pastures: he leadeth me beside the still waters. He . . . ."

Eventually, Ivan could not avoid the screams that preceded his death.

Chapter IX

Sarah sat down on an open spot of ground between two wigwams and yelled. "I hate you! I hate all of you! You're mean and nasty people!" She pulled up her knees and buried her face in the folds of her skirt. Her father was dead and the only family she had left in the world was Jessica. There was no comfort in that thought.

The night before, she cried herself to sleep curled up next to Charlotte, and woke up hungry. After lying still for a few minutes she realized she needed to go outside and relieve herself. She went to the flap that covered the door to the wigwam. The sun was up so she went out and walked to the edge of the village to hide behind a bush. As she walked back to the wigwam she smelled food cooking and followed her nose. The cooking smells were the same as the ones of the night before, and they brought back memories of her father tied to the pole.

When Charlotte woke up and realized Sarah was gone she hurried out to look for her. Sarah was sitting on the ground sobbing like her little heart would break. A few children stood by silently watching this strange, white girl who was crying like a baby.

"Sarah, Dear. Please come back to the hut. Someone will bring us food soon and you don't want to miss out."

"I don't care. My daddy's dead. Those bad Indians killed him," she sniveled.

"I know, but we mustn't talk about it here. Come on. Don't make me have to carry you."

Sarah looked up at Charlotte, then at the children standing around staring at her. She stuck out her tongue at them. "I hate you! I hate all of you!" she yelled again.

"Sarah. I'm going to spank you if you continue to talk this way. You will only bring harm to yourself, and maybe to the rest of us. Now, come on." Charlotte pulled Sarah to her feet and practically dragged her back to the wigwam just as two women brought food and water to them.

Sarah went to the bench where she had slept and curled up crying. Charlotte put Sarah's bowl of food in front of her and gently stroked her arm.

"What's the matter with her?" Jessica woke up and looked at Sarah. "At least you weren't beaten with sticks. I'll be scared for life!"

"Jessica. Be quiet." Mrs. Vause commanded, and Jessica glared at the woman as she wolfed down the boiled meat and vegetables. Mrs. Vause shook her head and whispered to Mary Engels "I don't know what will become of that girl. Poor, Sarah. Come sit by me, will you? How you must feel in this hostile place, you poor dear girl."

Sarah picked up her bowl and moved over to sit next to Mrs. Vause. She sat up and put her feet on the woven mat that covered the floor and using the same wool blanket that covered her at night, wrapped it around herself as best she could leaving her arms free.

"They beat you up, didn't they? They beat up everybody that ran by those people yesterday cept me and Charlotte. They're mean, bad people, and I was getting to like Chief Gray Fox." She sniffed a bit, wiping her nose with her dress, then continued, "I thought he would be nice to us, but he's just as bad as all the rest. Then they killed my daddy." She sobbed as she put a piece of boiled meat into her mouth.

"Your father was a very unhappy man. He's in heaven now with your mother. Together, I'm sure they are watching over you and would want you to be as brave as you were on the trail."

"It's hard to be brave when you're all alone."

"My dear girl. You have us." In spite of her pain Mrs. Vause reached out to put her arm around Sarah's shoulders.

Sarah looked at the cuts and bruises on Mrs. Vause. "Does it hurt very bad?"

"It's better this morning. I think most of my injuries are bruises." She looked inside the blanket and down at her naked body. "Oh, my God." She wrapped the blanket more tightly around herself.

"What is it? Is it bad?" Sarah looked at her with frightened eyes.

"It's not too bad. I look worse than I feel." The bruises Mrs. Vause suffered had already turned purple; some so dark they were almost black. The cuts were gray-green where the poultice was still stuck to the wounds and reddish where blood had seeped through.

Soon other women entered and cleaned everyone's wounds adding more poultice. Their clothing was returned, dumped in a pile on the floor.

Mary Ingles held up her petticoat and exclaimed. "It looks worse than I remembered from last night."

Jessica shed a brief tear for the pathetic change their trials had caused. She became aware of how much weight she had lost. Her ribs and hip bones protruded through skin that was now tight over bones with little or no padding left. "I look like a scarecrow. If we ever get to go home again, nobody will want to look at me. No one will want to marry me after this."

Mrs. Vause replied, "Be glad you're alive. Our bruises and cuts will heal in time."

Chapter X

Peter and two other captives went to the river to bathe. "I wish they'd tell us what they plan to do with us." Captain Smith spoke as he removed his uniform.

"I wish the same thing. We be sittin' around for three days now. Our cuts be healin' up okay and my bruises be more yellow than purple." Peter examined his arms.

The captives were all still wearing their own torn and dirty clothes, but had been allowed to swim and wash in the river. They were carefully watched by at least two braves at all times. A morning trip to the river was the only exercise they received. The rest of the time they were required to stay by the wigwams assigned to them.

"Early this morning I saw two women take the slave, Tom, to the river and scrub him all over." One of the men chuckled. "Did they think they could wash his black skin off?" The others laughed briefly.

Peter finished swimming and was pulling on his pants, his one remaining piece of clothing. "I saw somebody talkin' to Chief Gray Fox earlier. They were lookin' at Tom and shakin' their heads very friendly like."

When the three men returned to the wigwam from their brief swim, they noticed that Tom was being led to the clearing and people were gathering around him. The captives were able to watch from near the wigwam, where the men and women gathered.

Sarah stood next to Charlotte, and Peter walked over to them. "What's goin' on?"

"Hello, Peter. Sarah says that the man standing next to Gray Fox is going to adopt Tom as his brother."

"His brother?"

"Yes."

"Sarah? Are ya sure you understood right?"

"Yes. My new friend, Little Squirrel told me."

"I see." Peter could say no more. Sarah had not mentioned her father after that first morning, and now she seemed to be making friends with a little Shawnee girl.

The ceremony was a simple one. Tom now wore the breech cloth, leggings and a pair of new moccasins. His broad, muscular chest was bare. His hair had grown out a little, and the sides of his head were shaved leaving a strip of hair over the top. As the chief spoke, he wrapped a bit of buffalo hair around Tom's left wrist. A few words were spoken and the ceremony was over.

All the captives had watched this strange custom take place and when it was over they went back to the wigwam sitting outside on the ground with their legs crossed. "Well, what's next?" ask William Pepper.

Peter replied, "I be watchin' the comin's and goin's at the council house, or lodge, or whatever they call that big, long building over yonder."

"What do you reckon it means?"

"I think they be debatin' what to do with us. They been meetin' every day since we got here."

Chief Gray Fox approached and pointed to several of the captive men. "You come." They got up and followed him to the center of the clearing. A few minutes later Peter watched as the chief gathered the women and led them to the center where the men were.

Sarah and Charlotte ran over to Peter and Captain Smith who had not been called out. Both girls were crying. "Captain Smith, they're taking my mother and Sarah's sister away from us. They pushed us out and said we have to stay."

"I want to go with my sister!" wailed Sarah.

"I want to go with my mother," cried Charlotte.

Captain Smith asked, "Charlotte, do you know where they're taking them?"

"No. They won't tell us anything,"

"But, they're leaving us here?" Peter looked at Sarah who was crying for the first time since her father's death.

Charlotte sobbed, "We don't know anything." They stood still and waited as the others were lined up. Charlotte ran to her mother and threw her arms around her. "Momma, Momma, I want to go with you."

"I'm sorry, dear." Mrs. Vause was also in tears, but trying to control her anger and grief. "It pains me to be separated from you." They held onto each other as tears flowed. "I begged Chief Gray Fox to let me take you, but he refused. He wouldn't even discuss it. Now, we both must be brave. We have no choice but to do as they say. It's for our own safety. Sarah will need you. You're all she has now. You must look after her as best you can."

"I will, but Momma . . . ."

One of the warriors pulled Charlotte away from her mother and pushed her to where Peter stood with Sarah and Captain Smith.

Peter put an arm around Charlotte and Sarah wrapped an arm around one of his legs. They stood by silently as the others walked away. Mrs. Vause held onto Levisa's hand, and even Jessica looked back at Sarah shedding a tear.

"Now, I don't have any family," cried Sarah.

"I'm sorry, Sarah." Captain Smith spoke quietly to her. "You'll have to think of Charlotte as your sister."

"Well. She is a lot nicer to me than Jessica was, but Jessica is kin."

Charlotte looked at Peter and whispered, "This little girl will be a Shawnee soon. She's already learned a little of the language. She's smart and learns quickly."

Charlotte and Sarah were pulled away early the next morning, Peter and Captain Smith continued to sit, waiting for whatever would happen. They were now the only two white men left.

"Mr. Looney." Sarah ran though the village and headed straight to him.

"What is it? Are those tears I see?" He gathered her into his arms.

"I have to tell you something."

"And what could be troublin' a little bitty lass as yourself?"

"Little Squirrel's parents adopted me. They didn't even ask me if I wanted to. They just dragged me down to the river and scrubbed me so hard my skin hurt. Then they threw away my dress and put this Indian dress on me."

"Now, how could that be bad?"

"But, I have a real sister. I have Jessica."

Peter continued to hold Sarah in his arms. "I'm sorry, Sarah, but Jessica will be livin' somewhere else, and maybe she'll get adopted by another family. It's good for you that Little Squirrel's family wants you. Now, in addition to Charlotte you'll have another sister."

"Two sisters?"

"Two sisters. Just look at you, dressed like a Shawnee girl, and your long hair tied just like Little Squirrel's. Try to be happy, Sarah. In many ways this is good news. They will treat you the same as they treat Little Squirrel. They will take good care of you."

"Will you stay here so I can talk to you?"

Peter reluctantly shook his head. "I'm afraid not. Captain Smith and I were told we be leavin' in the mornin'. We don't know where they'll take us, but I'll know where you be. And besides, Tom is here. You can always talk to him."

"Yes. I know, but will you come back and see me?"

"I don't know if I can, but you will always be right here," and he put one hand on his heart as he put her down.

"Peter." Charlotte called to him, and he watched as a very different Charlotte walked toward him.

"I wanted to tell you that I have also been adopted by a family here. Their only daughter was married not long ago and they need me to help with the chores."

"How do you feel about that? Is it okay with you?" He looked at her in her new Indian dress of soft deerskin. Her long brown hair was parted in the middle and each side was tied with strips of deer hide. Silver bracelets encircled her thin arms. "You've got rosy cheeks. I hadn't noticed before. In fact I've never seen you look more beautiful."

"They are very kind to me, but I had no choice in the matter. Now that my white relatives have been taken from me, I suppose I shall have to make the best of it. I will be around to help look after Sarah."

"I'm glad for Sarah's sake."

"We are forbidden to speak English, but they have allowed us to come and say goodbye."

"Don't forget your English, Charlotte."

"I won't, but Sarah might forget in time because she's so young. As for my father, it's been so long since we were captured, and he hasn't found us yet. I don't even know if he is alive."

"I wish we were stayin' longer, but Captain Smith and I will be leavin' first thing in the morning, I don't know where they will take us."

"I'm sorry to see you leave."

"Don't forget that Tom is here. You all take care of each other."

"We will." Charlotte reached out and touched Peter on his arm, and he took her hand and held it for a moment. Then, she turned and took Sarah by the hand and walked away to where two women were waiting for them.

Peter and Captain Smith were told to stay by the wigwam, and this morning they were not allowed to go to the river. The sun had been up only minutes when four Shawnee braves appeared before them leading two extra horses.

Peter looked around him, "Captain, have you see the girls?"

"No, I haven't. They'll be okay, Peter."

"I know, but I wanted to see them just one last time before we left."

"It may be too early for them to be out. Don't worry about them. Their fate is now in the hands of God and these Shawnee."

The two white men rode side by side as they headed north. Peter turned to look behind him and saw Charlotte waving with one hand and holding Sarah's with the other. He waved back but was too far away to see the tears streaming down Sarah's face. From a distance they looked like two young Shawnee girls with long brown hair.

Chapter XI

Four young braves accompanied Peter and Captain Smith as they rode north to another Shawnee town. Peter had thrown away what was left of his torn shirt and by now his skin was quite tanned from the sun. His hair hung straight with no ribbon to tie it in the style of most Colonials. Now, with black hair and black eyes, he was beginning to look more Indian than white. The pony he rode was a spirited, husky, brown stallion, but after a few miles he settled down and walked.

Before turning north the six men traveled west until they reached the Little Miami River and followed it. Mid afternoon of the second day they reached another Shawnee village.

"That be a short journey. I thought we'd be ridin' for a few days at least."

One of the braves looked at Peter and scowled. "We not stay here. We eat. We sleep. When sun rise, we leave."

Peter whispered to Captain Smith. "Lordy be. I didn't reckon on him speakin' English."

The two captives were given something to eat, but they had to sleep outside with only a blanket for each of them.

Before daylight Captain Smith shook Peter's shoulder. "Wake up. The Indians are stirring and they'll be ready to leave soon." With no food offered to them, they again mounted their horses and rode north along the river.

"Talk to me Peter. My mind keeps running around in circles. I don't like to think about what awaits us in the next village." Captain Smith looked over at Peter who was so relaxed the Captain wondered if he was asleep. "I worry about the women and girls we left behind. What will happen to them?"

"Sorry Captain. I reckon that's the difference between a captain and the simple farmer I be. I try not to think about them too much, but little Sarah comes to mind the most. I think they be okay. I was thinkin' of me Ma and Pa. I worry if they be okay."

"I understand. I wonder if I shall ever see my wife again. She had to face losing our son at the fort. I hope he was buried before she had any knowledge of what happened to him."

"Yes, sir. That be a very bad sight to see."

"Did you have a girl you left behind?"

"There be one I fancied, named Margaret Lauderdale. Don't know if she'll be interested when I return, assumin' I do."

"Is she by any chance related to James Lauderdale?"

"She be his daughter."

"I know her father. A good man. He'll do well."

Peter looked around studying the change in geography. "This land be flatter than any I be used to. So much sky." They watched the clouds roll by as their ponies followed the two braves. "This be good farmland. Settlers be comin' this way one day. Already they be pushin' into western Pennsylvania. It be only a matter of time."

"The Indians are fighting the English, with the French by their side."

"And after the French finish fightin' the English, who will lay claim to all of this?" He spread his right arm out in an arc taking in the entire countryside. "The Indians have the right but that won't stop the settlers for long."

"Yes, as the English come, so will the Irish, Dutch, Germans and more. The French can't keep them out forever."

"Yes, sir. I reckon that be the case. I don't rightly know. I be just a simple farmer and hunter. I be thinkin' of my Ma and Pa, too. They have to know we be alive. My family been friends with the Cherokee for years, so I think they know I be smart enough to stay alive." He was silent a moment, "I be certain Ephraim Vause gathered a rescue party but I ain't so sure it'll do any good."

As Peter was growing up he had many occasions to listen whenever the Cherokee visited with his father. The Looney Ferry was a major north south crossing over the James River, and the Cherokee used it as much as his neighbors.

Peter held no hope of anyone traveling so far from home to rescue anyone, certainly not him. He knew he would have to make the best of his situation, whatever that might be. So, he took note of the territory as they traveled. The skies remained blue with only small puffs of clouds. With such a view into the distance it would be easy to see storms approaching. But, he took note of the low lying, rolling green hills covered with lush vegetation and trees hugging the streams and creeks.

After a few more days of travel they crossed the Upper Sandusky River and turned north-north-west. In the distance he saw a hunting party, and by late afternoon they reached another town. As they grew near he saw at least several hundred wigwams and children out playing. As Peter, Captain Smith and the four warriors rode into the town people stood aside and silently watched them.

Peter looked at them, smiled and waved to the children. Once he bowed and smiled at a young woman who stared at him. The rest of the time he studied the layout of the town as they entered.

The center of the town was dominated by the large council house, larger than the one in the first village. They dismounted, then were led into the building and told to sit. A few minutes later the chiefs, council members and other elders entered and took their seats.

"Welcome. We were told of your coming."

One of the braves looked at the man sitting cross legged on the ground, flanked by the elders. "Thank you, great chief of the Shawnee." He looked at Peter and Captain Smith. "Chief name Askuwheteau. In English it means He Keeps Watch."

Peter and the Captain sat across from the chief and though Peter looked at the chief and smiled briefly, Captain Smith stared defiantly at him. No one said anything for several minutes. Then the door opened and a short, rounded French commander entered the large room. He greeted the chief and the elders, and then turned to face the two captives. "Bonjour."

Peter and Smith looked at the Commander who was dressed in an immaculately tailored blue uniform with its gold trim. He spoke a few more words to the chief then turned and addressed the two captives.

"You are Captain Smith?" Smith opened his mouth to speak, but the Commander's hand went up and he stopped. "You realize you are a prisoner of war, Captain?"

"Yes. I know." He kept his composer. He had not been badly treated and had even made this last part of his journey riding rather than walking. He had been well fed and had no reason to fear the Shawnee in spite of their reputation. He also still wore his uniform, though stained, and his stockings torn.

The Commander looked at Peter. "What is your name, young man?"

"Peter Looney of Augusta County, Virginia."

"You've come a long way. Have you been treated well?"

"Yes, Sir. I be treated very well. Me wounds have been nursed and they healed well." He wasn't sure the later part was necessary, but he hoped to establish some well-being.

"Are you a member of the King's army?"

"No, Sir." Why tell him he was a member of the militia unless he really needed to.

"You look almost like an Indian. You're well browned by the sun and your eyes are as black as your hair. You even wear your hair as many Indians do. Are you part Indian in blood?"

"No, Sir. Manx thru and thru."

"Ah, Manx are you. They are a lot like the Irish are they not? Many Irish have fought with the English."

"Not where I come from. We consider ourselves American."

"So, you would never fight for the English?"

"Not I, Sir. Nor any of me brothers." Peter kept a steady gaze, as he lied to the Commander.

"You have many brothers back home in Virginia?"

"Ten that are living, sir."

"What happened to the others?"

"Me oldest brother died this last February." A sadness appeared in his eyes as he thought of his brother, Robby.

"Sounds like a large family. Any others?"

"Me parents and two sisters."

"You fought at Fort Vause. Why?"

"I was told it needed defendin' against the Indians."

The French Commander said a few words to the chief and without looking back walked out of the council house. Peter watched from the corner of his eye and wondered why the captain wasn't also questioned.

Chapter XII

Two French soldiers appeared inside the council house and looked at Captain Smith a moment before motioning for him to stand up. They looked him up and down noting his dirty uniform and worn out boots. Then one of them grabbed him by the arm and led him outside. Unsure what he should do Peter stayed put and watched. Captain Smith looked back at Peter but said nothing. The look on Peter's face was full of sympathy. Words were not needed. Captain Smith expected the worse as a war prisoner, but as a Captain he hoped for the best.

Moments later the chief rose to his feet and the Indians around him also rose. Chief Askuwheteau motioned for Peter to stand up and then took him gently by the arm and led him outside. The bright sun momentarily blinded Peter, but his eyes adjusted quickly as he walked with the chief.

Fires had been lit throughout the village and the smell of cooked meat was welcoming. His mouth watered as he inhaled the aroma. He quickly forgot the other smells made by horses, dogs and humans living in close proximity.

Two older squaws took Peter away from Askuwheteau and led him to the river. Confused, Peter looked at the chief who looked at him with a sly grin. "You go. They bring you back to my home."

Peter went with the two women but had no idea what was in store for him. For all he knew they were about to drown him, but figured he could break away if he really needed to. They first pulled his pants off, the only piece of clothing he had left. His momentary embarrassment brought a bright red color to his face, but the women didn't seem to notice. They then led him into the waist high river. This water was cooler than at the Scioto Town but the day was very warm so the water was refreshing. That was before they began grabbing fists full of sand to scrub him all over until his brown body turned red. On the shore stood a third woman holding what seemed to be folded up deerskins.

This be what they did to Tom. Now, I understand. He thought no more of fighting his way clear and allowed them to finish scrubbing him from his face to his feet. By the time they finished he stopped being embarrassed. Once they were satisfied with the job done, the two women led him out of the water to dry off. They dressed him in a breechcloth, leggings and new moccasins. He smiled at the women and bowed. Their eyes opened wide in surprise but they smiled briefly and led him away.

Askuwheteau's wigwam was just like the ones in the other village. There was a buffalo robe over the door that had been pulled to one side. There was a fire outside with an iron pot hanging from a cross beam supported by two thick sticks. The pleasant aroma of stewed meat and herbs met Peter's nostrils and he inhaled deeply hoping he would be eating some of it soon.

"Squaw is Red Bird. She very good cook. Now, you sit." Peter was pleased that the chief spoke English. In his hand was a pipe with a long stem. He smiled and motioned for Peter to sit down next to him. Other men appeared and gathered around them forming a small circle.

The chief held up the pipe, lit it and blew smoke out into the air a few times before passing it to Peter. Peter had watched the Cherokee use this form of ceremony, but this was the first time he had ever been asked to join. He took a small breath at first to test its potency, and then a larger pull. He too blew the smoke out into the space between them.

"The braves that brought you here say you are good man. From this day you are my brother. We will call you Wematin." He reached out to take Peter's hand and tied a strand of buffalo hair around his left wrist. "You eat with my family, sleep in my house. Perhaps you take a woman for your wife and make a home with her. Have many children. Grow up Shawnee." He smiled and patted Peter on the knee.

Peter didn't know how to respond and was relieved when the chief's wife served bowls of tasty hot stew and pieces of cornbread. Askuwheteau's wife then fed the others. The chief's friends stayed and chatted for some time. *This be a small celebration, and it suits me fine.*

Peter enjoyed the cool north-easterly breeze coming off Lake Erie as he ate and studied his new brother. Askuwheteau was probably fifty years old. His wife was much younger with two small boys. Peter guessed she was a second wife, a little plain but straight and tall. The two little boys, three and five years, were active and ran around naked playing with their toy bows and arrows.

As the days went by Peter learned more about the village. He worked at learning the language, mostly from Askuwheteau's friends as they came to talk with the chief.

Peter was full of questions and Askuwheteau politely answered them while also explaining that it was rude to ask questions. "But how else will I learn, if I don't ask?" The chief laughed in response.

Peter joined the other men as they went to the river to bathe each morning. He steeled himself to endure the cold water, and after a few weeks realized he could tolerate it rather well. He sharpened the hunting knife given to him by the chief, and used it to shave each morning. Shaving the side of the head seemed to be an individual choice and he preferred not to. His straight, black hair had grown below his shoulders which was the same as many of the warriors.

In wandering around the village he discovered a trading post on the northeast side next to the river. The trader was a big burly man with a young Shawnee wife who carried her baby wrapped in a blanket tied across her shoulder. "Hello. Do you speak English?"

"Oui. I speak good English. But, you not Shawnee. You white man?"

"Yes. Peter Looney from Virginia. I've been adopted by Askuwheteau as his brother. They call me Wematin."

"Wematin. I am happy to meet you, Wematin. I am Pierre Le Beau." He held out his hand to Peter. "Chief Askuwheteau very good man. You lucky, Wematin. Very lucky. You make good Shawnee. You come see me. We trade sometime. Come anyway. I like visitors."

"Thank you, Pierre. I'd enjoy visiting with you."

One evening as Peter and Askuwheteau were sitting outside the wigwam talking with a few older braves, Peter noticed a young squaw walking past carrying a bucket of water she held balanced on one shoulder. As she walked by she looked at Peter who could not help but stare. Her hair was pulled back and tied on each side with rawhide decorated with beads. He didn't have a chance to get a good look at her face but her large dark eyes and long lashes made a definite impression. He wanted to see more.

"Who is that girl?" He whispered to the chief.

"She Nuttak, sister to Askook, daughter of Lalawethika. He very old. She take care of him."

"Tell me about her."

"Her mother died of fever four winters ago. I do not think Askook will let her marry while father is alive. He very mean. You must stay away from him." The other braves shook their heads in agreement.

"That's too bad, but couldn't she marry and still take care of her father?"

"She could. It is her right. Askook not want her to. If she marry he have to find his own place. No woman want him. He be disgraced without a woman to cook for him."

"It sounds complicated but still, you're married with two little boys and you have allowed me to live with you."

"You are new to our ways. It is okay for many people living in one house. It is not impossible, but Askook different. We let people live as they wish. Must respect other people."

"Except for Askook."

"Now you understand."

Peter thought about Nuttak but knew better than to ask any more questions about her. His background was based on a man choosing a wife, but he quickly understood that in the Shawnee world the husband would be chosen by the woman. Then he wondered if Nuttak would ever want him? If he hoped to escape back to his own people he'd better not get too involved in the lives of the Shawnee. But, would that be possible?

Chapter XIII

"Mr. Vause. We can't go on like this. The men be tired and hungry. We ain't et for three days." Josh looked at the worn and haggard face of Vause. Josh was just as worn and he had been tying his pants tighter around his waist. Vause's rescue party had been following Levisa's trail for four weeks now, and men had been deserting almost daily. It was another night with nothing to cook, nothing to eat. The remaining men lay on their blankets looking at the multitude of stars. Such a sight would normally be very welcome, but this night it only reminded them of all they had left behind.

Earlier, fifteen men had turned back, some with expressions of sorrow and others just stealing away in the night. Vause's arguments had fallen on deaf ears.

"I can't blame the men for turning back. Everything I own is what's on me. I hope they find their way safely. With fifteen men we still have a chance, but Levisa's clues are all we have to go by." Vause found one more tree with her name written on it.

"She's one smart girl, Mr. Vause. I sure hope she be okay." Josh Miller was still holding out hope of a future with Levisa, if only they could find her.

In the morning there were ten left. Five more disappeared in the dark. When they reached the Ohio River the party stopped. "Mr. Vause, how you reckon we'll get across that?"

"I'm not sure, Josh. I've heard of the Mississippi but I cannot imagine one bigger than this." He dismounted and walked to the bank to contemplate their next move.

"Do you think the horses can swim that? How you figure the Indians got across?"

"I don't know about the horses. Maybe they can, but that's an awful wide river. I'm thinking they must have had canoes buried along the bank. Fan out and look. Maybe they left one or two."

"Hey, there's tracks here. This ain't where they crossed, Mr. Vause. We'll have to follow these tracks to see where they lead us. Maybe they did have some canoes."

"Okay, let's go." When they reached the place where the Indians had crossed they found the ground torn up with tracks, but no canoes.

"Well, there's nothing for us to do but build a raft, so we'd better get busy cutting down some trees." The sharp sound of the hatchet against hard wood rang through the hills surrounding them and birds scattered from every nearby tree. "Remember, the raft has to hold a couple of horses too."

The work required a different set of muscles and in their emaciated condition it was slow work. Some of the men chopped until it was too dark to see which way the trees would fall. Only then did they build a fire. With all the trees they felled there was more than enough fire wood.

Two of the men went out to hunt for food and returned after dark empty handed. "All that racket cuttin' trees and timbers fallin' done scared off every four footed critter within miles. We better hope we can fish in the dark. That'll be all we can hope to eat for supper. I'm so weak from hunger now; I'd eat a skunk."

Two men approached, each carrying a string full of fish. "What you got there, Josh? Why they ain't hardly big enough to throw back."

"They may not be very big but they're big enough. From the looks of that fire and nothin' cookin' on it, this be a sight better than what you brought in. You better pitch in and help us gut these things."

With only ten men left, Ephraim Vause was sure that if the grumbling meant anything some of those would also disappear. He was just as tired as his men, his arms ached and he had blisters on his hands from using a hatchet. But, each night as he lay on his blanket waiting for sleep to come he saw his wife and daughters. He would continue until he either found them or was forced to turn back by some force greater than himself.

"I'm not going to cross that river." Josh heard a few of the men whisper.

"You aren't going to leave us after all we been through are you?"

"I aim to head back while I can. Once we cross that river there's no turnin' back. A man alone can't cross a river that big."

It took another day and all the rope they could make to complete the raft. Three men walked their horses on and one held the reigns while the others used long poles to guide and push the raft. "Pull on that pole. It's trying to take us down river."

"I'm pulling as hard as I can."

"What we need is a long rope so we can pull it across like a ferry."

"Well, we don't have any more rope."

It was even more difficult for the third man to steer back across the river for the next few men and horses. "Sure wish I knew how those Indians did it." Vause spoke as he and Josh stepped onto the raft.

One man took the raft back across the river for more men and horses. Of the five men yet to cross, only one agreed to go. The others had decided to return home.

"Are you the only one comin'?" He asked.

"I'll help you get started across. We've got our muskets and enough powder and balls. Besides, we can move faster if we ain't tryin' to track."

"God be with you. If you see my family, tell I'm okay," Johnny asked.

The men watched as the raft re-entered the river. "Johnny, look out for that log." But Johnny didn't see the log until they collided. "Johnny. Johnny." Men were yelling from both sides of the river as the raft lurched with the bump and both men and horses went into the river.

The horses swam for the opposite shore, but when the men resurfaced they had been washed further down river. "Help. Help." Johnny yelled, his voice faint, but there was nothing anyone could do. The raft went spinning down the center where the current was faster. "Johnny, grab the raft. Grab the raft." But Johnny couldn't hear them as the raft floated further away. Finally, both men disappeared.

"Damn. Damn. Two good men lost and all because of me." Vause was almost ranting.

"Nobody blames you, Mr. Vause. None of us is good swimmers."

"The horses could swim. I should have had each of us hold onto the horses and let them take us across. They'd be alive but for me."

"Please, sir. We'll go along the shore. Maybe they got out down river a ways." With wanting to do something, no matter how hopeless, men on both sides of the river mounted up and searched the shoreline. When night fell and they couldn't see any more they stopped and made camp. The fear of being found by Indians prompted Vause to keep a cold camp that night.

The next day Ephraim searched for more signs from Levisa, but north of the Ohio River he found nothing. "There are the same syca-more and beech trees, but I've looked at every one of these and I don't see her name anywhere."

"Maybe she wasn't able to write her name, but they did leave tracks and what looks like a regular trail. This has got to be the right river. If we follow it maybe there's a tree she was able to write on."

"Okay, Josh. We'll follow this river."

"Yes, sir."

Chapter XIV

Every day the Shawnee washed themselves in the river that ran beside their village. The women and men swam in different areas and at different times according to their own schedules. If the women needed to wash clothes they used that time to also wash themselves. As some of the older men sat in shallow water rubbing their bodies with the fine sand, Peter preferred to swim. He didn't like rubbing sand on his body. When he returned from his morning swim he noticed Red Bird was cleaning out the wigwam.

"I'm hungry, Red Bird. How come there's no food?" He noticed there was no pot hanging over a fire. There was no fire. He hoped she had put something aside that he could eat.

"We not eat until festival tonight."

"There's a festival? What festival is that?" Peter stared at her, totally confused.

Red Bird shook her head as she gathered an arm load of broken pots and old clothes, "Askuwheteau not tell you? Today is Green Corn Ceremony. We celebrate the first corn of the season. You make him tell you."

"Oh. Like a harvest festival?" Peter was relieved that he understood. "But, what do you do with those?" Red Bird tucked a bundle under one arm.

"These no good. We clean house. We make new clothes now. Old stuff get burned," and Peter watched as she walked away and joined other village women, all with arm loads of stuff walking to one common trash heap.

Peter turned to look at Askuwheteau who sat outside smiling to himself. "Askuwheteau, what's going on?"

Askuwheteau looked up at the confused look on Peter's face. "It is a sign of inward renewal. Old things get burned. We make new. I waited for you. We drink the black drink together. Come. Sit."

"What's the black drink?" Peter looked at the two gourds that sat on the ground next to the chief.

"It is ritual we must follow at corn ceremony. Here, we drink together." Askuwheteau picked up the gourds and held one out for Peter. The liquid was indeed black, but Peter had no idea what it was. Like many things in the village it was one more that was new to him.

Peter looked at the black liquid and took a sip. "This tastes awful." He looked at the kindly old chief. "Do we have to drink it?" The chief ignored his question and motioned for Peter to drink it quickly. Peter followed his lead downing it as fast as possible. He then shivered a moment as if to shake the awful stuff away. Askuwheteau nodded his head and smiled at Peter but said nothing.

They sat quietly in the warm sun as Peter wished he had something solid to eat. Swimming had made him hungry and the thought of waiting until evening to eat wasn't a pleasant thought at all. What was he going to do with himself while he waited?

A few minutes later he ran for the woods. On an empty stomach it didn't take long for that black stuff to do what it's intended to do, although Peter didn't know that. It found its way back up faster than it went down. When he had completely emptied his stomach he staggered back to the wigwam and lay face down on the warm ground. He turned over onto his back and glared at Askuwheteau who didn't look like he had moved a muscle, but his face looked drained and worn.

"You should have warned me about that vile stuff."

"You would refuse to drink it. Now we are purified of all minor sins." The chief sat very still and smiled at Peter. "There will be great feast tonight. Then you feel better."

"I look forward to that." He wondered what minor sins he had committed aside from asking too many questions. He wanted to say he couldn't wait for the evening when he could put something solid into his stomach, but he was afraid that comment would not be understood.

He still thought as a white man, and wondered if the day would come when he actually thought as a Shawnee. *I could never think like these people.* He still planned to leave in the spring, after the last of the snows. He wasn't sure how, only that he would.

He noticed Nuttak walking toward him. She carried a basket of corn on her back with a strap that crossed her forehead, leaving her hands free. He watched her move gracefully as if the basket were nothing. Her long black hair was tucked behind her ears revealing silver earrings that gently touched her smooth tawny neck as she moved. Her eyes caught his and showed a flash of recognition and delight. When she smiled her full lips parted showing straight white teeth. Her skin was flawless, and her dark eyes were outlined with full black lashes. She wore a simple deerskin dress that ended with fringe below her knees. Her feet and arms were bare.

He had followed Askuwheteau's advise and stayed away from her, but seeing her walk over toward him caused a little stirring in his stomach that had nothing to do with the black drink. She stopped and looked down at Peter and laughed. "You sick? You have pale face, paleface."

"What are you going to do with that corn?" In spite of his misery he welcomed a conversation with her no matter how short.

"This corn for feast tonight. We not eat before that."

"Oh," Peter groaned. He heard her laughing as she walked away and he watched as her narrow hips swayed with each step. *She's even good to look at from the back.*

At last, it was late afternoon and the ceremony was about to begin. Peter followed the chief and his family to the clearing in the center of the village. The chief was dressed in his finest. He shaved the side of his head and put three turkey feathers in his hair that stood up above the crown. Two of the feathers were in shades of tan to black, but the third feather was died a dark red. His deerskin leggings had fringe down the sides decorated with multicolored beads of red, white, blue and yellow forming a pattern next to the fringe. His moccasins were also decorated with the same colored beads. On his arms were silver amulets and a necklace of silver hung around his neck.

"Askuwheteau? What should I do?" Peter asked in a quiet voice, because he felt every bit the outsider even though he was dressed the same as most of the other men.

"You do nothing. You sit by drummers and watch." The chief answered and pointed to a spot on the ground at the edge of the circle.

The people of the village were gathered in the center around a large fire chatting among themselves. The chief walked slowly over to the fire and raised his arms up over his head. The people grew quiet. The entire village watched in complete silence. Even the little children were quiet.

Askuwheteau looked toward the sky and spoke in Shawnee. "Great Spirit, we thank you for the corn that grows in the fields. We thank you for the rain that waters the fields. We thank you for the sun that helps the corn to grow. We thank you for a good harvest." As he spoke he turned to the north, east, south and west.

The drummers began beating on their drums. Peter was so startled he jumped, then quickly covered his ears and sat back down.

"Lord a' mighty. They could a caused me heart to stop," he exclaimed, though no one heard him over the noise.

The dancers, both men and women danced around the fire in rhythm with the drummers and sang as they danced. "Heh ya ha ya. Heh ya ha ya." A few had gourds filled with seeds or pebbles, and they rattled in time with the drum beats. The pattern varied little, but continued until all the dancers were tired. When the drums stopped the dancing stopped.

Three young girls came forward and, with the chief beside them, dropped kernels of corn and small bits of tobacco onto the fire. The chief came forward with another prayer of thanks.

Another dance began and Peter was better prepared as the drumming began. "It feels like they be poundin' on me. I feel it in me stomach." Askuwheteau came and sat down beside him. He had danced the first dance, but now he watched. Nuttak's father, Lalawethika came and sat beside Askuwheteau. Lalawethika was old and his arthritis made dancing impossible but he always came to watch.

Peter looked at the chief. "They sure know how to hop around." Askuwheteau just smiled.

The dancing went on for hours, and Peter began to wonder when he would be allowed to eat, but soon he began to smell the sweet aroma of cooked corn. At last, the dancing ended and everyone could eat. Peter approached Nuttak as she helped dish out the corn. Each person held out a bowl to her. "Nuttak, I saw you dancing. You must be tired." He noticed the moist glow on her forehead and little beads of perspiration on her upper lip. He wished he could touch her and wipe it away.

"My spirit was spent. Now I am renewed." She smiled and moved away to fill another bowl with the corn she helped to cook. Peter had forgotten to bring his bowl so he hurried back to the wigwam to retrieve it. When he returned to the cooking fires Nuttak was waiting for him. "I fill your bowl." She took his bowl from him and filled it. He wondered if this small jester held some silent message. Then he wondered why the thought would even occur to him.

The ceremony continued for two more days, each ending with more dancing and eating but no more black drink.

Chapter XV

Of the thirty five men that left Fort Vause six weeks ago only two remained and they were deep into Shawnee country, north of the Ohio River.

"Mr. Vause. We about done all we can do. What if we're found by Indians? They be just the two of us."

"I'm not turning back, Josh. I don't expect you to stay with me. But, I'll keep on trackin' 'til I find my wife and girls."

"Well, I reckon I'll stay with you, sir. I ain't got nothin' to go back to neither."

"I hope this trail leads us to something. Levisa hasn't marked any of the trees on the north side of the Ohio, but maybe we just haven't found it yet."

"Maybe they done found her out and kept watch on her so she couldn't," replied Josh.

"I only hope that's it. I've no idea what river this is, but this trail is about as much sign as we'll get."

Both men rode weary horses as they moved north. Ephraim Vause was as weary as the horse he rode. Every day he prayed he would find something to keep up his sagging hopes. He needed his wife back. He wanted his two daughters back. He silently and secretly wasn't sure that Josh would be the most suitable husband for Levisa, but he wouldn't worry about that now. They hadn't found food in the past two days.

There weren't even nuts or berries to eat, and he didn't dare shoot his rifle for fear of alerting an Indian hunting party. At least there was grass for the horses. After two days on the north side of the Ohio they were confronted by three young warriors on horseback.

"We come as friends," spoke Vause as he halted his horse and held up both hands.

"Why you come?" One who spoke English asked. He looked at the two emaciated white men. They were wearing clothes that were little more than rags.

"I come looking for my wife and two daughters." Vause waited while the Indians spoke among themselves.

"Two white girls live here. They not be sisters," responded one of the Indians.

"Could I talk to them?" Vause asked. His hope was alive again and he silently prayed that he knew them.

The Indians seemed to consider the request. "Come." They all turned and Ephraim Vause and Josh Miller followed two of the warriors. The third warrior followed with his rifle at the ready. They dismounted in the center of the village where their horses were taken away. Vause looked worried and confused when he saw them leave.

Sarah was playing a game with Little Squirrel and two other girls who had become friends. When she saw the two white men riding into the village she recognized them and ran into the corn field to get Charlotte. "Come quick." When she got hold of her arm she spoke in a quieter voice. "Your father and another white man are here."

Charlotte put the basket on her back and hurried to the center of the village. When Mr. Vause recognized the girls he tried to run toward them, but stronger arms held him back.

"Charlotte!" He yelled. "Sarah!"

Charlotte's heart beat faster, and she wanted to run to him, but she knew she would be punished if she showed much emotion. She put her basket down and walked quietly to the Shawnee brave who was holding Vause. "He is my white father. May I talk to him?" The warriors parted, but they stayed close and kept watch. The one who spoke English stayed close enough to listen.

Vause wrapped his arms around Charlotte and hugged her close to him, tears running down his cheeks. "My dear Charlotte. You're safe.

I prayed you'd be safe. Where are the others? Where is your mother? Levisa? Are they here?" As he spoke he tried to look past the warriors who looked as if they would pounce on him.

"They are not here, father. I don't know where they are. Everyone, except Sarah and Tom were taken to other villages. Perhaps the chief knows. We might be able to ask him."

"Are you treated well?"

"Yes, we have been treated very well. Sarah speaks Shawnee very well now, learning from her adopted sister and her new friends." She looked at Sarah's bright face and smiling eyes. "She even seems happy here." Sarah wrapped both arms around Charlotte. "I will try to speak to the chief on your behalf. First you must rest and have something to eat." She spoke to the warriors who frowned and grunted disapproval.

"There aren't many people in the village right now. The warriors left to fight with the white settlers and they are not happy to see two of you ride into their village."

Charlotte sat at an acceptable distance from her father and Josh Miller as they talked. "Please tell me everything you can, Charlotte. I want to know about your mother and sister."

"They were all well when they left here a week ago. They were treated well."

"One week ago? I missed them by one week?" Ephraim Vause was almost in tears at the thought. He wiped his dusty face with a dirty rag he kept in his pocket. It did little good.

"I'm sorry, father. I know you're upset" She leaned forward and spoke very quietly hoping the Indian guard couldn't hear, "but we have no control over our lives, even though they treat us well. They don't like for us to talk to you. This is why they watch so closely. Did you find Levisa's name on the trees?"

Vause understood and lowered his voice, "that's how we were able to track you to the Ohio River. From there we found tracks and a trail along this river that we decided to follow."

"This is the Scioto River. Levisa is very brave, but I was afraid for her. Mother spoke little on the trail but she was always encouraging. If there is a trading post attached to the village they may have found employment sewing shirts. I have made a few myself. The trader pays in goods." She held out the silver necklace she was wearing.

"Then you are well treated?"

"Yes. I have missed you Pa and I have longed to return home, but I see no way for that to happen. I must stay here and make the best of it. I have been adopted and the family would not allow you to take me away. Tom is here, but you won't be seeing him. He has joined the warriors in their fight against the whites." She started speaking a little faster half expecting someone to call a halt to their meeting.

"Tom? My slave, Tom? He's helping the Indians to kill our people?" Vause stood up and in his agitation paced back and forth. "Oh, Charlotte, this is so upsetting to me. I'm your father. They should not try to break up families like this."

"Oh, Pa. Don't make this any harder than it is. You are my white father. I have a Shawnee family now. They won't let me leave. They may kill you to keep you from taking me away. You must understand. And I've got to stay for Sarah's sake. I promised Ma. Sarah needs me."

"Stay? You don't mean you would live here always?"

"Yes. That's what I mean. I see no other way."

"But, these are savages."

"Yes. Her father was burned at the stake the first night we were here."

"Burned? You see how savage they can be? They must let you come back with me."

Charlotte stared at her father. "You don't understand, Pa."

"But, Charlotte. They aren't even Christians." He tried to keep his voice under control but after six weeks of hoping and longing and searching he found it almost impossible.

"No. Their religion is very different."

"I cannot accept this. You must return with us. I am your father. I must insist you come." He started to pound his fist onto his knee for he had nothing else to hit.

Charlotte looked at her father. Her expression told nothing of her feelings, but inside her heart was being torn apart. "Are you willing to pay a ransom?"

"A ransom? We came in peace. We only ask that they return my family to me. Is that asking so much?" Vause was almost yelling now in his agitation.

"Father, please, lower your voice. I seriously doubt that will happen. But, if you wish to continue to hope, we will wait and see what the chief decides. In the meantime you must be patient and calm. Don't do anything that will upset them."

The next morning Charlotte was called to the wigwam of the chief. He looked at her as she stood in front of him. He was the brother of her adopted father and knew how much they wanted to keep her.

"You are good Shawnee girl. Your family cares much for you. They would never let you go. You must tell this white man he may be your white father, but you are Shawnee now and you have Shawnee family. You must stay. You ask about the other whites. I do not know which villages they were taken to. There are many Shawnee towns and villages. Maybe they were traded to another tribe. I do not know the answer to that."

"Yes. I understand." She went out of the chief's wigwam with a heavy heart. She had longed to be returned to the white settlement, and it hurt to think that she would never see any of her family or friends again. *Best not to think about that.*

She went to the open place where the two men had slept, watched over by four warriors. They had been given food to eat the evening before, and were being fed again. It was probably the only food they had eaten in several days.

"Good morning, Pa. I have come from the chief's wigwam. There is no way to know which village took them in. They were separated from us and very likely separated from each other. They could be at any one of a dozen villages. It is even possible they were traded to another tribe."

"What do you mean traded?" Vause was exasperated to think he had come this far and still know nothing. His hopes were being shattered and with them his soul, for without his family he felt too devastated to go on.

The chief came out of his wigwam, walked over to Vause and stood in front of him with his arms folded before him. He had an angry look in his eyes. "You go home. Girl Shawnee now." He was annoyed that this white man was being so persistent. He wanted him gone, now.

"I would like to take my daughter with me."

The chief shook his head, "No! She Shawnee now. She stay." The angry look on the old chief's face told Vause he was not open to negotiation, but he had to try.

"I have money. I'll buy her back."

"Not want money. Girl Shawnee now. You go away."

Charlotte stood close enough to hear their conversation, and she understood the look on the chief's face. She had resigned herself to staying with the Shawnee. The night before she had cried very softly and quietly longing to go home and knowing that it was impossible only made the longing more difficult to bear. She knew her father loved her as much as Levisa, but uppermost in his thoughts would be his wife. Now, she turned and silently walked away. The pain of saying goodbye to her father would be impossible to control. It would be better if he left and said nothing. A few tears escaped from her clouded eyes as she returned to the corn field, and she avoided the other women as she tried to bring her emotions back under control.

Ephraim Vause could not believe his ears. His reluctance to accept what he was hearing took awhile to penetrate. He finally realized he had best leave while the option was still open. He looked at Charlotte and watched her walk away, knowing he would never see his daughter again. Their horses were returned to them and he slowly took the reins, handing one to Josh.

"We'll be leaving now, Josh." Ephraim said no more as he mounted and nudged his horse toward the south side of the village and onto the trail through the woods nearest the river.

"Mr. Vause. How are we gonna find Levisa? What happens next?"

"We're going home, Josh. No more questions, please." Vause replied quietly. He let the horse follow the trail, for it was impossible to see as the tears ran down his cheeks.

Chapter XVI

Peter was enjoying his morning swim, and was glad his brothers had made sure he learned at an early age. There were several other men in the water and still others sunning themselves on the bank. Askook was one of those in the water and he swam over to Peter and pushed him into deeper water. At first Peter assumed Askook wanted to speak to him, but instead he grabbed Peter around the neck and pulled him under water. Then he hit him on the side of the head and again in the stomach. Peter managed to kick his way free and came to the surface, coughing and sputtering.

When he could catch his breath he yelled, "What'ya doin'? You tryin' ta drown me?"

"You stay away from Nuttak. She not marry you." Then after punching Peter in the stomach again he swam quickly back to shore. Peter coughed and sputtered again fighting to get air into his lungs. When he got out of the river he asked one of the other men.

"Did you see what he did?"

"Askook bad man. You stay away, you be okay."

"Thanks for the warnin'." Peter stumbled back to the wigwam, but said nothing to anyone. Even though he had spoken very little to Nuttak, he went out of his way to avoid her for the next several days. He wanted no trouble with anyone. There were plenty of others who were friendly, and he still wasn't sure of his place among these people.

The rest of his days were spent in practice with a borrowed bow and arrow, wrestling with his teacher, Big Thunder, throwing competitions and the occasional games.

One afternoon he was sitting outside the wigwam sharpening a hunting knife. "Askuwheteau, will you teach me how to make a bow and arrows? I have watched the others. I would like to have my own so I may join the hunters."

"You go to Chogan. He is best maker of bows and arrows. He has been working on new bow for you." Askuwheteau smiled sheepishly showing two missing teeth in his brown and wrinkled face. His dark eyes twinkled.

"Did you ask him to make one for me?"

"I ask him many suns ago, when I saw much progress in your shooting of arrows."

"How can I thank you, Askuwheteau? You are very kind." Peter couldn't help but like his older Indian brother. He really was a good and generous man.

"You thank me by being good hunter. Bring many deer, bear, and elk to lodge."

"I will. I promise." Peter looked forward to the day the Shawnee would allow him to join them on hunting trips. He had prided himself on being a good hunter whenever he went out with his brother, Absalom.

He grew stronger each day, and enjoyed the competitions and the challenges. The more proficient he became the more he gained respect, and made friends of the other men. Askuwheteau saw the changes in Peter and felt proud. His hair was long and straight black, and his body had turned brown all over. He could even run in his bare feet.

Peter watched the women returning from the fields where they worked the crops. As the weeks passed and the harvest was ready all the women carried baskets to the fields and gathered the corn, and other grains to be stored for the winter. They also went into the woods in small groups to gather nuts, berries and herbs to be dried for seasoning meats. Their baskets were large and they carried them on their backs with a carrying strap that went across their foreheads, leaving their hands free.

"Wematin. Come." Peter had watched Askook approach and rose

to greet him. Several young braves had followed. "We fight. You and me. We see who is stronger. Who is best warrior."

"You want to fight me?" Peter had never been challenged before, so this came as a big surprise. He had been learning to wrestle with his teacher, Big Thunder.

"We fight. I show you who is best warrior." He pulled himself up, standing tall and proud in front of his friends.

Askuwheteau heard this exchange and watched as Askook took another step closer to Peter. "You must fight him, Wematin. But remember, he fight mean. May the Great Spirit be with you."

Reluctantly, Peter put down the arrow he had been fixing and stepped toward Askook. He stopped three feet from him and looked him in the eye. Askook was a few inches taller than Peter, but about the same weight. Askook lunged at Peter and threw him onto the ground. Peter wrapped one arm around Askook's neck and tried to grab his closest arm. Askook was quicker, and Peter was rolled over onto his stomach. Big Thunder had taught him well, but he wasn't as fast as Askook. He managed to turn around and wrapped his arms around Askook's neck and pushed with his feet. This threw Askook over Peter's head and onto the ground on his back. Askook kicked Peter in the groan, rendering him momentarily helpless.

A ring of onlookers had assembled and Big Thunder pushed himself into the ring. He grabbed Askook by the back of his hair, pulled him close and whispered into his ear. "You fight fair. If not, you fight me next." He held Askook back until Peter had time to recover, then he let go.

Askook was now so angry he roared. Peter just stared at him, waiting for his next move. When it came Peter countered and threw Askook to the ground. Then he pounced on top and sat on him pinning his arms to the ground.

"It's a draw, Askook. I have no quarrel with you."

"You not marry Nuttak." Askook growled, then spit in Peter's face.

"Okay. I will not marry Nuttak. Not as long as you live." He got up, wiped his face and walked away.

Later, he watched as Nuttak carried her basket back from the fields. It was no coincidence that she passed near the wigwam where Peter was living. It was rarely a coincidence that he would be sitting outside the door. They did not speak but Peter watched her as she walked by with her eyes on the ground in front of her.

"Askuwheteau, Nuttak looks very sad whenever I see her. Is it because of Askook?"

"Nuttak angry with Askook for fighting with you."

The longer Peter lived with the Shawnee the more he learned about them as a people. In many ways they were no different from the Cherokee or the whites he knew. They took care of each other. The young helped the elderly, elders taught the children, and playfulness and compassion was common throughout the village.

There were other things he was learning as well. Unlike the whites, young boys at a certain age were taken from their mothers to live and be raised by another family member, an uncle or cousin. They were taught not to be too attached or separation in death would be more intolerable. They were taught to be stronger in heart as well as in body. In a way Peter was being taught the same lessons, but he was not learning it as well. His heart yearned for the family back home even as his body grew stronger.

Askuwheteau had been called to the council house for the War Dance and he took Peter with him. "You stay in back and listen. Do not speak."

Chief Askuwheteau sat with his council members and the War Chief, Machk. They sat quietly around the sacred fire inside the lodge, smoking the sacred pipe. No one spoke until the pipe had been passed to all the council members. Every face held a solemn expression. Peter could not read their thoughts even though he stared at Askuwheteau.

Chief Askuwheteau spoke slowly and quietly in Shawnee to the council. "The French have commanded us to go east and kill all white people that live on our side of the mountains. These white people have not honored the treaty that says they will stay on the other side. They build strong houses and bring cattle into our land and keep them behind a fence. We have talked for two long days and now it has been decided that we must do as the French have told us. Machk, our warrior chief will bring great honor to us. Machk, go with the blessings of the Great Spirit."

Machk stood and answered, "We will bring honor, and we will bring many white scalps."

When the war chief finished, Peter thought that was surely the end and he started to get up. But before he could leave, mothers, wives and sisters of the warriors entered and took their places when the Pipe Ceremony ended. Among the women was Nuttak, and Peter stared at the intense look on her face as she concentrated on the dance. Two men sat in front of the dancers holding gourds filled with pebbles. The gourds were shaken as the women began chanting. Warriors danced around the sacred fire and at regular intervals the men let out a sharp, short whoop. Inside the circle stood two old warriors painted in black and red with terrifyingly painted tomahawks and scalping knives. When the dancers jumped and shouted they waved their tomahawks and knives. When they finished the dance they all let out a blood chilling war cry. The hair on the back of Peter's neck stood up and he felt a cold chill run down his spin even though the evening had been very warm.

Outside the council house the Shawnee continued dancing around an even larger fire. Two more warriors danced and darted around the fire, imitating a raiding party. They waved tomahawks and yelled. Shots were fired into the air, and warriors whooped as they danced. More firing and whooping was accompanied by the steady beat of drums and rattles.

Peter wanted to be far away from this for it seemed to be a dance of death. But a feeling of morbid fascination kept him near enough to see, but only from the darkness. He watched Askook as he had danced among the warriors, knowing he would be going on this raid. The party was ready to go out and kill white people and Peter felt the bitter helplessness of being unable to do anything but watch. He also knew that Askook relished the idea of killing as many whites as possible and wondered how many other warriors were as eager.

The next morning Askuwheteau looked at Peter's sad face. "I know what questions you wish to ask. I will answer. The Shawnee do not want white people building on lands given to us by the Great Spirit. White people promised to stay on the other side of the long mountains, but they have broken the treaty. You know that your own people trespassed into our lands. Now, our warriors will kill these English who dared cross those mountains."

"Thank you for telling me, Askuwheteau." Peter pondered the conflicting emotions in his heart and head. His head told him that the Shawnee were right to protect their lands. Treaties had been agreed to and broken. But as a white man he also knew of the hunger for land and doubted that an Indian raid would stop them. They would break those treaties when they could see miles and miles of open country lying to the west, waiting to be cleared and farmed. In the minds of the white men there was more than enough land for everyone. Others don't consider the needs of the Indians as being worthy of consideration. Many of them want only enough land to raise their cattle and plant their crops. But the Shawnee and the other tribes depend on the vast open land to provide them with wild meat and fish. As the white man kill the game there is less for the Indians. Peter sat for a long time pondering this problem for which there was no answer. It was enough to make his head hurt.

After the war party left there were only a few men left in the village, mostly old men. Two of them asked Peter if he would join them to hunt turkeys as they would be easy to carry and the need for meat was a constant one.

"Yes. I would like to hunt with you. It would be a good test of my skill with my new bow and arrows." The next morning the three men left at dawn.

They walked for three hours along the river, and Peter was surprised how easy and relaxed he felt as he followed the other men. When the sun was high one of the men said to Peter, "You wait here to shoot turkey we scare out of bushes."

Peter readily agreed and sat down on a rock to wait. From a small bag hanging at his waist he pulled a few pieces of pemmican. The meat had been dried by Red Bird and he chewed it slowly savoring the seasonings she always added. When he finished he stepped to the edge of the creek, knelt down and pulled handfuls of water to his mouth. A few more handfuls were brushed across his face, and the cool water was refreshing. He knew it must be late September now. The days were still very warm with few clouds and beautiful sunshine but the nights were growing colder.

As Peter waited he stared into the brush along the creek but no turkeys appeared. In fact there was only the sound of a breeze in the tree tops and the gentle murmuring of water as it flowed over rocks in the creek. "Now, where be those men? They be too far to scare up a few turkeys." He got up and walked into the woods, moving very carefully and quietly. About thirty yards ahead he found a turkey sitting contently on a rock in a small spot of sun. He knew that with a bow and arrow it would be a long shot. He may not have been as experienced as the other men with a bow and arrow, but he was a hunter and he wanted that turkey. He hid himself behind a tree and very slowly placed the arrow on the bowstring and pulled back. The arrow hit the turkey squarely through the bottom of its stomach. Another inch lower and he would have hit the rock instead. "Wow! Saints be praised!" He hurried over and picked up the bird and slung it over his shoulder.

He whistled a call, a very weak whistle. His brother Absalom had despaired of his ever learning the simplest calls. He yelled. But there was no response. It was then that he realized the men had played a trick on him.

"What a fool I be. Still. I wonder if they returned with any turkeys," and he headed toward the creek and followed the path back to the village. When the other men, who had been waiting to see what he would do, saw him approach with the bird slung over one shoulder they were the ones to be surprised.

"So, you thought to leave me in the woods, did ya?" He handed the turkey to Red Bird and sat down across from the men and laughed. "How many turkeys did you bring back?"

"You okay, Wematin. Next time we not play trick." They all laughed, and as each of them left they tapped him on the shoulder and smiled. Peter smiled back.

"I guess that was their way of testing me." He looked at Askuwheteau's face.

"My brother okay," the chief spoke as he smiled showing his missing front teeth.

The warriors who had ridden away to fight the English and whites would not be expected for another two weeks. Peter walked along the river always heading west. He dared not head east for fear someone would think he was leaving for good and he wasn't ready for that. With the coming of winter it would be best to wait until spring. It was still in his mind to leave and return to his family, but he was not foolish enough to attempt such a journey with winter approaching. It would be difficult enough to find food and shelter along the way.

Peter's favorite spot of all the beautiful places along the Raisin River was on a flat rock overlooking the water. From here he could see for several miles. He watched the fish swimming around in the quiet eddy along the shore. He thought about catching fish, but first he just wanted to sit and watch as the sun moved higher into the sky. The shadows changed color and grew smaller. He had only been sitting there a few minutes when he quickened. There were footsteps on the path; light footsteps. He turned slowly and saw Nuttak approach. He watched as she climbed onto the rock and sat down beside him. His heart leaped. He had often thought of her in spite of Askook's warnings. She smiled briefly and sat very still looking at the river.

"I saw you leave village, but you not carry bow and arrows."

"I didn't plan on huntin'. I suppose I should ha' brought 'em just in case I spotted a deer or another turkey."

"I heard about trick they play on you. Those old men can only talk and play silly games."

"That's okay. I had a good day, and we all laughed about it."

"They will talk for many moons. You good sport. Bringing back turkey made everyone like you better."

Peter smiled to himself, but could not think of anything else to say, so he sat still and bask in the warmth of her nearness to him.

Chapter XVII

Peter had begun to hunt with a few of the younger me still at home in the village. On one of these hunts he happened to run into the path of a large, black mother bear. Without realizing it he had placed himself between the bear and her cub. He let out a shrill scream that brought the others running. Before the bear could be killed Peter received several claw marks. The bear ripped his shirt and tore his quiver loose, scattering his arrows onto the ground. The bear's claws also ripped at his back and arm leaving deep gashes and blood covered his arm and back. Now he needed to repair the quiver and replace the arrows that were broken when the bear trampled them.

Ice had formed along the edges of the river, so Peter swam quickly and hurried back to the wigwam and the warm, heavy buffalo robe. Red Bird rubbed more salve on his back and arm. "You learn everything hard way, Wematin." She shook her head. "Maybe someday you hunt bear and bear not hunt you."

"That's very funny, Red Bird. But, at least the bear and the cub were killed, and you have a fine new bear skin and bear oil to show for it."

"Yes. Good to have bear oil, and bear meat. Now, you hold still while I put on medicine."

At mid-day dogs were heard barking. That usually met someone was coming into the village. Peter and Askuwheteau rose, went outside and followed the crowd that was gathering in the center. The warriors were returning from their trip east and each one carried scalps on his belt, but soon the yelling and whooping was joined by screams and wails from the women in the crowd. Of the forty-two warriors that left only thirty returned. Some had been buried, but not all. Hearts were broken. Wives, sisters, friends and mothers wailed.

"Askuwheteau, this is frightful news. The warriors who have lost a friend will want to kill me for being white."

"No." Askuwheteau grabbed Peter by the arm. "You Shawnee now. They see you as Shawnee. You walk and talk like Shawnee. You brave like Shawnee." They stood at the edge of the crowd, but Peter knew there would be a council meeting and soon.

When the leader of the war party went into the council lodge later to tell the story of what had happened Peter hid in the background. Everyone gathered around the sacred fire inside the lodge and waited. Chief Askuwheteau stood up before the assembly and held his arms outstretched. "We are greatly saddened by the loss of many brave warriors. We honor them. Many have gone to join their ancestors in the great hunting grounds in the sky. Before us are those brave warriors who have returned to us and we rejoice in their return after more than one moon away from their home. I ask Chief Machk to tell us of their journey."

The War Chief, Machk, stood straight and tall. In Shawnee he addressed the gathering. "Fathers, uncles, brothers and friends; I bring to you news of what has happened in the east. Many whites had crossed the mountains and entered land they promised not to enter. They have built strong houses made from big trees. Trees they cut down to make homes that will last for more winters than a man can breathe the air. They plant seeds in the ground to grow corn to feed the beasts called cattle. They build fences to keep these cattle in one place so they may not wander freely. They build these places along deer trails and rivers so the deer cannot travel as they once did. They kill the animals of the forest and take fish from the rivers. They use our hunting grounds." He pounded his fist on his chest for emphasis. "These are grounds left to us by the Great Spirit. These are grounds we have fought to keep, and grounds we must share with other tribes."

Machk stopped for a moment to look around. Every face was turned his way and remained silent, waiting for him to continue. "We burned many cabins and took many scalps. We killed their cattle and took their horses. We took some captives and left them at Scioto town. Our warriors were brave and fought well. They have many scalps to show as proof of their bravery. But, my people, do not think that this will stop the whites. They break treaties and more will come. This is why we are friends with the French. They will trade our furs and give us presents, but the French do not build fences, and bring cattle. They do not build strong houses out of trees. It is true the French build forts, but they stay in their forts. They do not tear down the forests we must depend on to feed our people."

As Peter listened, he was glad he understood enough Shawnee to know what was being said. As he watched he noticed Nuttak slip outside the lodge and he left to follow her.

"Nuttak. I didn't see your brother. Did Askook return?"

"He is not among those who have returned." She looked at him but there were no tears in her eyes. She showed no expression he could read.

"I'm sorry for you and your father."

"Father will be saddened, but I cannot find the tears that should fall from my eyes."

"Your father will be very sad."

"Yes. He will be sad." She turned and Peter watched as she walked away.

The meeting had ended. Now, there was a celebration for those who had returned, and as the elders smoked their sacred pipes, others danced around the fire in the center of the lodge. Still others went home to mourn in peace.

Peter's head was a battle ground of thoughts and images. He ached for the white families who had been killed or captured, their homes and dreams gone up in smoke. But, he was helpless to do anything about it, and his feelings of helplessness tormented him. When Asku-wheteau returned from the council house Peter had gone to the river to sit. He let his mind wander to his home and family back in Virginia. He wondered if they were well, or if another raiding party had burned their farm. Were they all alive? There was no way to know. *Virginia may as well be on the other side of the sea for all the help I be to 'em now.*

He ignored the footsteps that approached from behind him. Nuttak sat down beside him. He brought no robe to cover himself as the night grew cooler; she draped her own buffalo robe over his shoulders to cover both of them.

"Why are you here, Nuttak? You should be home giving comfort to your father."

"He was not stupid. A bad spirit haunted Askook. Father knew that someday Askook would try to be braver than he really was, and would be killed. My father is sad but not surprised."

"But, he was Askook's father."

"Yes. And now he knows that without Askook to stop me I am free to marry. My father would be pleased to see me marry and give him many grandchildren. He has been wanting this for some time."

"I hope you will find the man you want." As Peter spoke he ached to put an arm around her, but didn't dare just yet.

"I have found him, but he does not want me." She kept her eyes on the water in the creek, not daring to look at Peter.

"I'm sorry, Nuttak," he whispered.

"You are sad tonight. Why is that?"

"I'm afraid that I will be blamed for the deaths of so many warriors." Peter's pain in knowing so many whites were killed would not leave him. He remembered only too well how much the family suffered when his older brother, Robbie was killed. They never were able to receive his body. He was buried where he was killed, only a day into the failed Sandy River Expedition.

"But, you were not there. They will not blame you. You are Shawnee now. You must remember. You are Shawnee. Not white." She desperately wanted him to think more like a Shawnee and hopefully forget his past.

Peter turned to look into Nuttak's eyes. The moon shone brightly and her eyes were moist and deep. He felt an almost hypnotic pull and he moved his face so close he could smell the breath on her slightly parted lips. In that instant he heard a voice calling him.

'Peter. Peter Looney, where be ya?' The voice was his mother's, and it rang as clear as a bell on the evening breeze. He pulled back with a start and looked around. There was no one there.

"What is wrong? Did I do wrong?"

"No. No. It's not you. I heard a voice. A voice in my head calling to me. I'm sorry, Nuttak. I must go."

"Where are you going?"

He was gone without answering her.

Chapter XVIII

When Peter entered the wigwam the fire had burned low. He put another log on and went to his blankets. Askuwheteau was snoring when Peter lay down on his own bench. Thoughts of his mother's voice returned, but in his mind's eye he kept seeing Nuttak's beautiful eyes. He could not deny his desire for her. Of course he wanted her, but he also cared enough to do nothing that would hurt her.

All the next day Peter walked along the river bank trying to think. Even though he carried his bow and arrows, his mind was not on hunting. He knew that Nuttak would make a good wife, but he was sure that marrying her was not the wise thing to do.

Finally, he dragged his feet back to the village and went to Askuwheteau to talk. "Brother, I have a heavy heart and don't know what I should do."

"Tell me what makes your heart so heavy." Askuwheteau smiled quietly.

"I like Nuttak very much and I know she would make a very good wife, but I'm afraid it would not be wise."

"Why would it not be wise? You have proven yourself to be a good hunter of animals for our food and skins for clothing. We do not ask you to kill the white people. There have been some whites who have turned against their own people. I have heard of them. Blue Jacket is one who was born white, but is now a mean man and fights against the whites. No one ask him to. Now he has become a chief. You are not like Blue Jacket. You are a good man, and that is why Nuttak wants to marry you."

"You think she wants to?" He looked at Askuwheteau with a heart that was beating rapidly.

"Red Bird hears all the talk among the women. Nuttak is yours if you want her." Askuwheteau spoke briefly allowing Peter to decide for himself.

"I must think about this some more."

"Why trouble yourself with so much thinking? Marry her and be happy. You will make her very happy." Peter thanked Askuwheteau and went outside. He stood beside the wigwam and looked around. The village was busy with women carrying baskets of corn, berries and herbs. Children chased each other, and young women carried babies on their backs. He watched as two hunters carried a deer tied to a long pole. Each man had one end of the pole balanced on his shoulder. Old men sat outside their houses sunning themselves. Peter saw Nuttak returning from the fields with a basket on her back, and he walked to intercept her.

"Nuttak. May I speak with you?"

"Yes, Wematin." She answered but continued walking.

"It would be good to marry you. I would like that, if it is also what you wish."

She put her basket on the ground and turned a radiant smile to him. "It is what I have wanted. It can be so in three days. I will spread the happy news." She put her hand on his chest and smiled again before picking up her basket. *Well, as easy as that?*

The next morning, Nuttak went to see Askuwheteau's wife. "Red Bird. I must ask a favor. I have no mother now and Wematin and I are to be married. Will you help me cook the dumplings and serve them two days from now?"

"I have been waiting for this day." She clapped her hands together and beamed at Nuttak. "I am very happy for you and I will be glad to serve in place of your poor mother." Red Bird put both her hands on Nuttak's shoulders and put her face close on either side.

"Thank you. I must begin making his new clothes. I have some deerskin that Askook gave me last winter." When she said this she realized how angry Askook would be, but he was no longer here to object.

"What about your own dress? I have no daughters. I will ask around. You must have a new dress. My aunt and sisters will be happy to help."

"Thank you, Red Bird." Nuttak returned to her wigwam with a happy smile.

Askuwheteau was waiting for Peter when he finished his swim the next morning. "Wematin, there is something you must do. I tell you because you would not know if I did not tell you how these things are done. As part of the wedding you must kill a deer and bring it to Nuttak. This you must do tomorrow."

"Am I to do this alone? I have never hunted alone." A worried look crossed his face.

"You must do it alone, and bring it back before tomorrow night." Askuwheteau knew this could be a most impossible task for his adopted brother, but hoped he would succeed.

"That is a difficult task. What if I fail to find a deer?"

Askuwheteau shook his head. "To fail means you are a poor hunter and would make a poor husband for Nuttak. Do not fail."

"I'd best leave before dawn." Peter began going over in his mind all the little things he must not forget.

"Yes. Long before dawn as the deer will be feeding at that time."

He looked at Red Bird who was working on the corn that would be cooked. She had borrowed three other large pots, and her aunt and sisters would come to help.

Later that day Peter watched as Red Bird and three other women filled three large pots set to boiling over fires outside the wigwam. "What are you cooking? You haven't cooked this before. It smells good."

"These are the dumplings we cook for your wedding. Everyone will come and fill a bowl. They take it back to their home to eat."

"They don't stay around and party?"

Red Bird looked at him quizzically. No. This not feasting ceremony, but happy time. I think many people will come."

"It sounds nice." Peter had no idea what all this meant, but he went along with whatever he was told.

"Nuttak is beautiful and a favorite of village. Many people will come." Red Bird looked at Peter hopefully, knowing the impossible task he must perform tomorrow.

Nuttak filled Peter's bowl that evening with the dumplings before helping Red Bird serve all the others who came to share in this special dish. But, each person brought his or her own bowl and carried it back home to eat. Peter sat outside the wigwam with Askuwheteau and they ate in silence as Peter watched Nuttak.

Later that night sleep would not come. He worried about finding and killing a deer on his first hunting trip alone. He watched the fire in the center of the wigwam as it burned down. When the fire was reduced to glowing embers he got up and added more wood. By the time Red Bird awoke to begin her daily chores the wigwam would be warm.

Peter gathered his bow and arrows, then wrapped his wool blanket around his shoulders and left the wigwam. He checked the position of the harvest moon and trotted the first half a mile. "Maybe I should a got up earlier. It be close to dawn now." He slowed down and began to walk carefully; trying to practice the careful steps he had been taught. "I gotta remember everything. I be disgraced in Nuttak's eyes if I fail."

Peter walked another two miles and the sun was up but on this day it was hidden behind clouds that had blown in from the west. *The breeze be in my favor. But I don't want rain"*

The day grew warmer in spite of the clouds. *I wish I hadn't brought this blanket. I should a known it would be an extra burden I don't need this day.*

On a low rise in a somewhat flat landscape Peter paused to look around. *Oh, what a beauty!* About half a mile away he spotted a buck with a beautiful rack of horns. *If only it will stay there. Not enough trees and brush for me to hide in.* He put aside his blanket and with his bow and quiver in his hands he lay down in the grass and began to crawl toward the buck.

Thank god for the breeze. He be up wind of me.

It seemed to take forever for Peter to crawl through the tall grass toward the buck. Every minute or two the buck would stop grazing and look around. Peter would stop still and wait until it lowered its head again. When he was finally close enough he lay still a moment feeling the pounding of his heart. Then he slowly placed an arrow on the bow and pulled back on the string. From a prone position he let loose his arrow. It found its mark, but not exactly where Peter wanted it. The arrow was lodged behind the shoulder and above the heart. The buck began to run. Peter jumped up and ran as fast as he could. He knew the buck would easily outrun him, but if it was fatally wounded it would fall eventually. He needed to know where that would be.

He ran until he thought he could run no more. Then he saw the buck. It had fallen in a cluster of bushes. Except for the white under the tail Peter might have missed him altogether.

"You are a beautiful beast. I hated to have to kill ya, but we need your meat and skin. Your horns be an extra treat. What am I doin'? I'm talkin' to a dead animal. Oh, I know I'm to give thanks to ya for allowing me to take your life so that the people can live. Well, I thank ya for lettin' me do this on this day of all days. Nuttak will be very happy."

"First off, I gotta rest a we bit before I can lift ya. Even then I hope I got the strength to carry ya." He looked around. "Oh, good god. Where am I? I was so intent on not lettin' him get away, I forgot to pay any attention to where I was goin'. I hope I can follow me own tracks."

Peter managed to get the buck draped over his shoulders and held onto the buck's legs, but now he had to walk several miles with it. "What I wouldn't give for a friendly hand to help carry this beast." He was able to follow his tracks for awhile, but then the rain began. First, it was just a drizzle that had not disturbed his tracks. But after walking about a mile the rain began to fall in torrents, and the wind blew hard at his back. He tried to ignore the rain, but without tracks to follow he focused on an object in the distance and hoped he was following a straight course. However, when the buck was running, it didn't follow a straight line.

"If I can get to the river, I think I be okay. Now, where is the river?"

Luckily this part of the country was open with patches of forest. "The river runs through much forest. I must follow that. But, this buck be heavier than anything I've ever had to carry in me life. A small doe would 'a served me purposes just as well."

After a while the rain stopped, but the clouds blocked out the sun.

"Okay. I been walking north, and I know I'm on the south side of the river. I must have run further south than I thought."

"I suppose I could cut up the buck and come back for part of it tomorrow, but I'd have to do a lot of work on him and hide part in a tree so the wolves don't get it. But, I don't really want to do that. I'd be more proud to present the whole thing to Nuttak. Besides, I wouldn't want to cut up the skin, and I don't care to skin the whole thing meself. I'd just botch it up. The women are so much better at that than me."

Peter trudged on, going more and more slowly. "The river. I see the river. It can't be too far now. Another few miles and I'm home. Home? My god, I just called the Indian village home. It ain't home. But, I've agreed to take an Indian wife. I don't know what I'm doing. But, I want Nuttak, and this is the price. One big buck for a beautiful Indian girl."

By the time Peter walked into the village, it was late in the afternoon and the sun would drop below the horizon soon. He almost stumbled as he made his way to Nuttak's wigwam. When he got to the door he called to her.

Children, women and a few old men had followed Peter, all chattering about the beautiful big buck he was carrying. Nuttak came out and looked at Peter and at the animal he carried. Word had spread throughout the village and everyone wanted to see Peter present the buck to Nuttak.

"This is for you." Peter dropped the buck on the ground at her feet, and then he fell to his knees in exhaustion.

"You have done well, Wematin." Her pride was shining in her dark eyes.

Her father put his hand on Peter's arm. "You are now a great hunter, and worthy of my daughter. I welcome you as the husband of Nuttak."

Peter was pleased. He rose to his feet and stumbled back to Askuwheteau's wigwam and collapsed onto his bench.

Chapter XIX

"Wematin. Wake up now." Red Bird called as she stood over Peter. "You married now. You take things and go to Nuttak's house. You not live here anymore." Red Bird laughed as Peter groaned, his back stiff and aching.

"I think I could sleep for a week."

"You cannot sleep. You go now." She spoke more harshly now, but with a little laugh.

Peter dragged himself up and rolled his buffalo robe into a bundle. His bow was still attached to the buck he carried yesterday, but he grabbed his quiver, his moccasins and left. As he walked over to Nuttak's wigwam, young girls stood in a group watching him and giggled. He was still too tired to care, but he forced a smile.

Nuttak and a few other women were busy cutting up the buck and drying strips of meat in the sun. The skin had been stretched and two women were scraping the underside in preparation for softening the hide.

He stood facing Nuttak. "I'm sorry I wasn't here sooner. Carrying that buck wore me out. Red Bird had to wake me up."

Nuttak smiled at him. "You my husband now. You sleep. My friends will help me with the buck you brought. Are you hungry? I have food for you." She put a hand on his arm and gently escorted him into the wigwam they would share with her father.

"I'm hungry."

"It is custom for me to give you bread first." She handed him the bread and a bowl of stewed meat. After eating he went to the bench they would share and fell asleep again. Nuttak looked down at him and smiled.

By nightfall, Peter had regained his strength, and his passion for Nuttak. Lalawethika went to his blankets after eating his evening meal. Peter and Nuttak sat quietly holding hands until Peter decided the old man was asleep and he couldn't wait any longer. He picked up Nuttak and carried her to the bench that was almost not wide enough for two people. He checked the blanket that hung from the ceiling giving them a little privacy. Then he began to kiss her, holding her close.

Complete isolation for the newly married couple was not possible with her father sharing the same wigwam, but Peter was happy with Nuttak. He only complained once.

"Wematin, you lived with Askuwheteau and Red Bird for several moons. Did you not think about them being alone? Perhaps they would have wanted more privacy than they had with you in the same house."

"You're right. I guess I never gave it any thought."

"We share the same bench and the same buffalo robes. We will manage all that you want."

"Well, not all, but it will have to do." He smiled and leaned over to kiss her.

Hunting took on a renewed intensity. The season was growing late and the hunters were out two and three days at a time. The women gathered the last of the corn and prepared it for storage through the winter. The kernels were stripped from the cob and stored in baskets buried in the ground. Berries and herbs were dried and stored. Meat was stripped, dried and stored in animal skins to keep it dry. At the far end of the council house where fur from their winter hunts would be kept, seeds and nuts were being stored. It was a busy time for the entire village.

"Tomorrow it will be time for us to leave for our winter hunting camp." Lalawethika was gathering a few things he wanted to take with him. "We will have two more families. We need young men to join you in the hunt. We have too few relatives so we must join two or three other families."

"Yes, father," replied Peter. Several families had already gone but he wanted one more trip to the river before they were to leave. "Where is Nuttak?"

"Nuttak with Red Bird. Red Bird help her decide what is needed for three families. We will live together in winter camp, and this be Nuttak's first trip away from village. The other families belong to Big Thunder. They are brothers and sisters. His sister, Sweet Dawn have two sons. Only one big enough to hunt."

"Who will be the other hunters?"

"Little Bear, Beaver, Gray Wolf and Keme. They be good hunters. You can learn much."

Peter turned away. Being told he wasn't as good as others still bothered him. He tried, but his efforts were mixed. Some days he could be enormously proud of himself. Then on other days, he was glad no one was watching.

He began rolling mats and buffalo robes. He also gathered his bow and the extra arrows he had made for the stay in their winter camp. With baskets full, and blankets and robes, pots and kettles loaded onto their backs they began the long trek through the woods and meadows to their winter camp along the Maumee River.

Chapter XX

The small hunting party trudged through the woods on their snow shoes. They had been walking since dawn over half a foot of snow. This was slow work, and Peter didn't dare let the others know how difficult it was to walk on snow shoes, but decided they knew anyway. It was almost impossible to keep anything from these men. They possessed a sixth sense that he lacked no matter how hard he tried. Maybe, he was trying too hard but relaxing in this cold was impossible. His fingers were freezing.

"This track of big buck, Wematin. You watch." Little Bear looked at Peter. He had made up his mind that Peter would never be a really great hunter, and didn't like having to teach him.

Peter was almost afraid to breathe. He had trapped one large buck but at least he would not have to carry this alone. He tried to relax but the more they followed the tracks the more excited he became. The anticipation before the kill was one of the aspects of hunting he enjoyed.

I can hardly wait. He could see that the track was made by a big buck. The signs were obvious, but Little Bear kept telling him things as if he was stupid and he resented this.

Peter had followed the four hunters along the narrow path of hoof prints left in the snow. They left camp at daybreak and walked quietly. The snow had not formed a hard crust that would crunch with each step of their snow shoes. They were confident of not being heard or seen, and the buck was up wind. All the signs were in their favor.

They followed the tracks for what seemed like a long time. Peter's fingers were stiff from the cold and he worried he would not be able to handle his bow and arrow. He made a fist and loosened it to work his fingers, and blew warm breath on his hands. A buffalo robe was draped over his shoulders and he carried his bow in his left hand with his arrows hanging loosely from his belt.

Another mile of tracking and the woods opened up to a natural meadow. On the near side a beautiful large buck with six point antlers stood quietly feeding. Two does stood nearby. Peter thought to himself, *Nuttak would love to have that soft doeskin.*

The hunters spread out, staying well back and downwind of the animals, moving carefully from tree to tree. It was a slow process to move close enough without frightening them. When they were close enough the leader of the party gave a signal and five arrows sped through the air at once. Four of them hit the buck and he began to run. The other two arrows got one of the does in the neck and she started running. The second doe was not hit, but frightened when the others ran and she disappeared into the brush.

"Now, we follow tracks." The hunters ran after the wounded animals, but their snow shoes slowed them down. "They leave good tracks, but not travel together."

Peter followed the wounded doe, and before long he realized the others had all followed the buck. This country was new and he didn't yet know his way very well.

It was only seven days ago that this small party of Shawnee made their winter camp on the Maumee River. The wigwam was snug and warm with three small fires burning continually inside the long building shared by all. Three families with five young men to hunt, shared the same wigwam with three smoke holes in the ceiling. Blankets were hung from the ceiling to partition the sleeping areas. Woven mats covered the cold earth floor.

Peter looked forward to warming his feet by the fire and the thought consumed him as he followed the tracks of the doe. He hadn't gone far when he noticed spots of blood mixed in among the tracks. "It can't be much further now," and he continued to hurry, certain of finding the doe waiting for him.

"Oh, no." He stopped short and ducked behind a tree. "Damn wolves."

Ahead of him, not fifty feet away, the doe lay still on a bed of red blood surrounded by five wolves, busily ripping her apart. There would be nothing left for him to take back. If only he wasn't alone. Two or more men could have driven them away, but one alone could not. He stood and watched. "They must have been watching the does while they fed and followed them here." The wolves devoured the animal in such haste it seemed to Peter they had not eaten in the past few days. He turned to follow his own tracks back to camp.

Peter had only walked a few hundred yards when he noticed the prints of a large cat next to his prints. He stopped and looked around then put an arrow on his bow string. He saw only the trees and the snow. The cat prints had followed his, turning away and continuing down toward the bottom of a gully. He went in the opposite direction and climbed up the small rise. *I hope she only wants what is left after those wolves finish.* He breathed quietly but could feel his heart pounding against his chest.

Peter now had no tracks to follow, but by staying on the ridge between the two gullies he hoped he would find his way back to camp. He was certain he was going in the right direction but the sun that had come out earlier for a few hours had now disappeared behind low lying clouds. *There be snow in them clouds.* He stood still for a moment hoping to hear the sound of other hunters, but the woods were so quiet. All he heard was his own breathing.

Snow. It'll cover me tracks. I must get back to Nuttak. She'll not know what became of me. Gray Wolf will accuse me of running away. He was upset when I married Nuttak. "No. Nuttak. I'll not leave ya." He yelled to the forest around him. He hurried on until the two gullies met and he crossed over to another rise. He didn't remember this spot and there were no tracks. Snow was falling more heavily now and the tracks would soon disappear. He searched the sky for signs of smoke. "Surely, I'll see the smoke from the smoke holes in the wigwam."

Peter saw nothing but snow, and it was falling so thick it cut his visibility. He looked behind him and his own footprints were rapidly disappearing. Behind him were five wolves and a big cat that he knew of and no place to hide. "I can't stop. Wherever I am I have to keep goin'. If only I'd paid more attention to landmarks and less attention to the tracks of that doe." He spoke aloud as if he wanted to be heard.

Peter tried to make a bird call. If any of the others heard him they would know him by his obviously poor attempt. He tried again, but no response. He decided to keep on trying. Surely, someone would hear it.

Just as darkness fell he saw something to his left. "A light." He walked toward it not certain it wasn't an enemy camp. He kept walking. "It be a lot further away than I thought. He walked closer. The light was like a pinpoint in an otherwise white wall of falling snow. Then he broke out into an awkward run. Nuttak was standing outside their wigwam staring off into the woods.

"Wematin? Why do you come from so far south of camp?"

"I . . . I was searching for the doe. It ran away."

"Where is it?"

"A pack o' wolves got to it before I could, then I found the prints of a big cat following me, and I didn't want it to find me so I changed my path. Why is there a fire outside?"

"You were lost. I make fire to guide you. Come inside. You are covered in snow. You almost white like the ground. I have saved some stew for you."

He wrapped his arms around her, and even through her robe he could feel the warmth of her body. "Good. I'm cold and hungry." He kissed her quickly.

"Oh. You frozen. Come inside now. My stew warm you up."

"And later?"

She refused to answer but laughed and took his arm and led him inside. He threw off the buffalo robe and stepped out of the snow shoes. Peter sat down close to the fire and held out his hands to bring warmth back into them. As his fingers began to tingle he pulled them back. He was forgetting to warm them slowly.

He watched as Nuttak scooped up the stew and handed him a bowl and he ate heartily enjoying the warmth of the food as it moved down into his stomach. As he ate the stew he watched her. Her deerskin dress hid the slight swelling of her stomach. Peter thought he had never been happier.

Nuttak's father sat next to Peter as he ate. "I was wise to say yes to this match. Nuttak happy. Better since little girl. You good husband. In time you be good hunter."

That evening the rest of the camp listened as Peter told them what had happened to the doe. "You bad Shawnee," laughed Gray Wolf. Peter had to agree.

The other hunters brought in the big buck and the women spent the next day cutting the meat and scrapping the hide. The snow fell all the next day, so the hunters decided to look to the care of their weapons and wait a day.

When the snow stopped there was a foot of it on the ground and now, a day later the men were out and as they walked it began snowing again. The day grew darker and they were miles from camp and found no game to shoot. They needed shelter for the night.

"Come. We go to cave I know. Maybe no bears inside. If bear sleeping inside, we have bear meat."

"That sounds like a good idea." The others agreed and they went off to find the cave, but when they reached it they were in for a surprise.

"Roof fall in. No bear here. We find different shelter for the night. Snow falling hard now."

"What a minute." Peter went into the overhang and began pulling out rocks.

"Wematin, you crazy man. Why you do that?" asked Gray Wolf.

"Come and help me. We can make a shelter for the night. Pile these rocks over there by your feet. We will build a wall and have a cozy place.."

"You make cave?"

"No. But with a fire under here, the rocks will help hold in the heat."

"Wematin." Beaver spoke. "You not crazy man like Gray Wolf say. You pretty smart for white man."

"Thanks. We can't stand up under here, but we'll be warm for the night and there be room for all five of us."

With a fire at the entrance they wrapped up in their robes and slept. In the morning they each ate some of the pemmican they always carried in their pouches.

The hunters had now been away from their camp since early the day before. So far they had no meat to take back. Outside their small shelter the snow had stopped and left them with well over two feet of it. The shelter was on the side of a low hill. They put their snow shoes back on and walked down to the bottom where they found tracks. "Deer? Asked Peter."

"Big deer, or little elk. Hard to see shape of track in so much snow."

"Should we follow it?" Peter asked.

"Big hunter want to follow elk?" asked Gray Wolf teasingly.

"Ho, ho, ho. Yes. Big hunter want to follow elk, or whatever it is." He wanted game he could carry back to the warm wigwam.

The others laughed and began the hike through the snow. They were lucky to be downwind of a large bull elk. "Little Bear will use rifle if we miss." He explained that Little Bear was the best shot among the five of them. Peter had witnessed Little Bear's expertise, and wished he also had a rifle. He knew he was just as good, but he hadn't been able to obtain one. He would have to ask Askuwheteau how to get one.

They followed the tracks into the bottom of the draw between the two hills. As they rounded the bend they were rewarded with one large bull elk with massive antlers. Still downwind the men ducked behind the nearest rock or tree and waited. The bull was busy rubbing his antlers against the bark of a tree and had his rump toward the men. Two men backed up and circled around to the left; two others circled to the right. On Beaver's signal four arrows found their mark and the bull elk ran about ten yards before falling down.

Now the work began and the bull was bled, gutted and quartered so they could more easily carry it back to camp. The meat was wrapped in deer skins they had carried for this purpose, and it took them most of the day to travel back to camp.

The women worked quickly and expertly as the men saw to their arrows and bows.

As Peter repaired his arrows and rubbed his bow with bear grease, he thought about how excited Absalom would be to know what he was learning. He thought to himself, *I sure do miss the folks back in Virginia, but I have a wonderful wife now and a new baby due in the spring. I best not be thinking on that.* He looked at Nuttak and smiled.

Two more moons of the winter hunt and they would be returning to the Shawnee town. Already the snows were less frequent and heavier. Spring would come soon.

Chapter XXI

It was late March and the hunters and their families were back in the town and preparing for the First New Moon of Spring Ceremony with a feast, rituals, and dancing.

"I not dance, Wematin. This child getting too big. I walk like duck."

Peter smiled and put his arms around her. "You walk like a princess. If you don't dance I won't either."

"You dance. You watch others. Do what they do. That is all. I have food to fix, and a new shirt I must finish making for you to wear. Now, leave me to my work."

Peter was lost among all the activity. He took up his bow and quiver of arrows and went hunting alone in the forest. During their winter hunting trip on the Maumee River he had finally succeeded in giving Nuttak the doe skin she wanted for the baby. The small hunting party of which he was a part had been successful in bringing in many deer, elk, and bear, plus three buffalo. The men still teased him whenever they had a chance, but he laughed with them. He was finding the Shawnee to be an affable people among themselves and he enjoyed living with them.

He was thinking more of his life with Nuttak and not paying attention to where he was going, something he still needed to learn. He had gone about two miles upriver when he spotted a lion sitting atop a boulder some six feet above the trail. The tawny color of his coat caught Peter's eye. He paused and waited to see what the lion would do. Would it challenge him, or simply walk away? He thought it odd that the lion would even allow itself to be seen. They were notoriously shy and recluse. The lion was about forty yards away, too far for a good shot. But, Peter's arrows were in the quiver on his back. He didn't dare make a sudden move. He also realized he was up wind, so the cat no doubt smelled him. Peter stood perfectly still, barely breathing. The cat turned and disappeared from the rock into the woods. But, where did it go? Peter stepped off the trail and put an arrow onto the bow string keeping his eye on the woods. New growth had begun to change the color of the forest. Among the browns there were now touches of green. Peter watched the ground on the far side of the path. If the lion tried to creep up on that side he would see it. It would blend with the dry leaves. If it crossed the path to his side it could have circled around behind him. He turned quickly to scan the nearer woods behind him. Not ten feet away he caught the white and tawny face with its distinctively dark markings across the eyes, nose and mouth. Then it hissed at him, a high pitched hiss that made his blood run cold.

Peter moved a little more quickly now, and pulled the bow string back hard against his cheek and pointed the arrow at the cat's head. Instinctively, Peter knew that cat was not going to back away and when it moved to leap the arrow flew through the air and caught the cat in the throat just as its forepaws left the ground. Peter stepped back holding his breath. The cat fell at his feet, and Peter heaved a sigh of relief.

"I gotta be more careful. The good Lord be on my side this day."

Peter picked up the cat and draped it over his shoulders. He walked back into the village smiling proudly as children gathered around him.

"Nuttak, come out. I got somethin' for ya." Peter called. Her father came out first and showed a toothless grin. Then Nuttak came out. Can ya do somethin' with the skin of this cat?"

Nuttak did not smile, but shook her head. "How you get that? They not attack people. They stay far away."

"Well, this one seems to have changed his mind. He got behind me and would'a jumped me if I hadn't turned around in the nick o' time. So, are ya sayin' you don't want this fine fur for the babe?"

"I not say that. Of course I want it." With that Peter dropped it on the ground and helped her skin it.

A few days later Nuttak had finished cleaning out the wigwam. Then all family fires were extinguished and a sacred fire was lit in the center of the clearing. The medicine man sprinkled tobacco onto the flames and chanted as he danced around it. He spread kernels of corn over the blaze and circled it again. When he finished chanting everyone joined together in a feast of corncakes and venison stew.

"Father, come sit with us." Nuttak called to Lalawethika who was too crippled with arthritis to dance any more. People too old or disabled sat and moved their heads in time with the drumming, and young mothers nursed their infants. Small children tried to dance along with older brothers and sisters.

Nuttak picked up a burning stick. "I can carry that for you," Peter said.

"It is a woman's duty to relight the family fire."

"Well. It seems the men are useless except for hunting."

"We depend on the men to keep us safe so we may care for the home and children."

"I look forward to our little one runnin' around."

"In time, Wematin. In time." Nuttak laughed. "In the morning we begin the planting."

"Are you sure you should be getting' down on your knees."

"I am Shawnee," Nuttak replied proudly. "Shawnee women strong."

A few days later Peter took three of the beaver pelts he had trapped during the winter and went to the French trading post.

"Ah, bonjour, Wematin." My friend has become Shawnee. I 'ave not seen you in many months."

"I have been busy. I am married now, and my wife expects a baby in another two months."

"Ah. A ba be? What can I do for the new papa?" He laughed and patted Peter on the back.

"Can I trade these beaver skins for a rifle and shot? Also some powder?"

"You want a rifle?" The smile left Le Beau's face and he grew serious.

"I can be a better hunter with a rifle than with a bow and arrow. With a new family I will need to bring in more meat."

"Humm. Let me advise you on one thing, my friend. Have Chief Askuwheteau buy the rifle for you. There be too many suspicious minds if you buy it for yourself. If Askuwheteau presents you with a rifle it shows he has much trust in you." Le Beau spoke as he put an arm around Peter's shoulder and they walked a few steps away from the open market.

"How can they doubt my loyalty?"

The trader shrugged his shoulders in reply.

Chapter XXII

The day was warm and many men sat outside their wigwams enjoying the midday sun.

"Askuwheteau. May I speak with you?" Peter stood before the chief and waited to be invited to sit down. His adopted brother patted the ground beside him as he blew smoke into the air from his pipe.

"Sit, Wematin. You look like you have big problem to solve."

"I wanted to trade some beaver belts for a rifle. I know I can be a better hunter with a rifle, but the trader would not trade with me."

"He be afraid to make me unhappy. If you want to hunt with rifle; use mine."

"I didn't know you had one."

"I have it for some time. I keep it wrapped in buffalo robe." He held up his right hand. "I get it for you." Peter sat warming himself while he waited. "Here. You take. Here is pouch of shot. But, I not have powder. It would not be good after so long a time."

"Do you think the trader will give me powder for a beaver pelt?"

"He should give you plenty powder and some shot for one pelt. Go to him. Carry the rifle so he knows you have one."

"Thank you, brother. I will bring in much meat with this and you shall have plenty to eat."

Peter walked back to the trading post. "Okay, Trader Le Beau. I bring a rifle that Chief Askuwheteau has loaned me. So I want powder and shot for this fine beaver pelt."

"So, he told you how much you should get for the pelt?"

"He did." Peter spoke more forcefully knowing the trading value of the pelt he carried.

"Trés bien. I hoped to bargain with you, but okay. I show you I am fair trader."

Later that afternoon Peter sat next to Lalawethika. He cleaned and oiled the rifle while his father-in-law smoked his pipe and stared into the fire as the rain outside pelted onto the roof of the wigwam.

Early the next morning Peter left the village with Askuwheteau's rifle and pouches full of powder, shot and two freshly baked corn cakes. "I'll be back before night." He kissed Nuttak and walked away into the woods. "I feel better with a rifle in me hand," he muttered to himself."

He followed no particular trail, but marked the trees to find his way back, something he learned during the winter camp. "I should not get meself lost again." During his hunting trips with Absalom he never got lost because Absalom was never out of his sight. As a result he learned a little but not enough.

The day began bright with a few clouds, but before long a drizzle began to fall and didn't stop for some time. Late in the afternoon he still hadn't found game to shoot, but he did spot a bear. *Oh, oh. This time of year that's bound to be a hungry mother. Now, where be her cub. I done got caught once before between a mother and her cub. I don't aim for that to happen again and me all alone.* He looked around but didn't see a cub. The bear saw him and stood up on her hind legs. After letting out a bone chilling roar she dropped to all fours and came running.

"Oh, my god. Climb a tree you damn fool before she gets ya." Peter scooted up a good sized tree, one he didn't think the bear could climb, and sat out on a limb too high for the bear to reach. "I sure hope you don't plan on coming up here after me." He tried to speak in a level voice, but his hands shook and his heart pounded against his chest.

The bear looked up the tree, and Peter sat as still as he could not making a sound. The bear put her paws on the trunk of the tree and began to pounce against it. *Is she trying to shake me out of the tree?* He didn't dare make a sound, but held onto the trunk of the tree until she stopped shaking it. Then very carefully he turned the barrel of his rifle around and pointed it at the bear. He pulled the trigger. There was only the faint click of the hammer. Nothing else. The tree was a tall pine, but the bear didn't fit between the branches so she didn't climb. However, she sat down on her haunches and waited. Peter stared down at the bear. "Now what?" He removed the powder and reloaded the rifle. This time it fired, killing the bear. "Whew!" Knowing what that bear could do to one lone man with a gun that wouldn't fire kept him shaking. "I was worried there for a bit." He carefully climbed down from the tree watching the bear in case it wasn't really dead. When he approached he poked it carefully with the barrel of the gun. Then he breathed a sigh of relief. "She's lost a lot o' weight sleepin' through the winter. I think she be small enough to carry."

Peter brought the bear to Askuwheteau and dropped it next to Red Bird's outdoor fire. "I want to talk to Askuwheteau."

"He in council meeting. He there all day."

"What's going on?"

"I not know. Many French soldiers come to meeting."

"I'm leaving Askuwheteau's rifle with you. He let me borrow it. I'd like to listen in on their meeting. I will go to the council house. I would like to know what they want." Peter left her and walked to the council house and crept in un-noticed. He sat in the back.

The French Commander was speaking to the village chiefs and sub chiefs. Peter didn't understand French, but the Shawnee words were understandable enough. *He wants war with the whites. He is demanding they go to Fort Duquesne, then to Fort Cumberland and kill the English there. I will have to ask Lalawethika where these forts are. I've not heard of them, and I pray they are not in Virginia.*

Peter was quiet that evening as Nuttak handed him a bowl of stewed bear meat. "Wematin, why you look sad? It good you brought bear home today. Red Bird say I can have fur for my son when he born."

"You sure it be a boy?" Peter worried but tried to remain calm and paid attention to her every word.

"I asked the Great Spirit to bring me a son. So, I believe it will be what I want."

Peter smiled, but said nothing. "Lalawethika? Do you know where Fort Duquesne is?"

"It is in the east. It is between two rivers, Monongahela and Alle-gany where they become the Spay-lay-wi-theepi. I see many snows ago. That is French fort. I not know why they want warriors. Maybe they need defend against British.

"And Fort Cumberland is on the Potomac River. I think I know about where that be, though I ain't never been there. I be pretty sure it belongs to the British," Peter continued.

"Our warriors be gone many moons." Lalawethika spoke between puffs of his pipe. "You must hunt."

The decision to send two war parties out at the same time took two more days of talking between the elders and the French. The French promised them all the spoils and payment for each scalp they brought back. They agreed to go and bring back these things they will take from the white people.

A large fire was built in the clearing. The warriors painted their faces red and black. They also painted their tomahawks, and when the drumming started they began to dance around the blaze.

"They be a terrifying sight to see with their faces all painted like that. They be scary." Peter was reminded of the same war paint that was worn during the attack on Fort Vause. "I think perhaps I go to our wigwam," he whispered to Lalawethika.

The strong hand that gripped his arm pulled Peter back. "Not wise to leave before warriors finish dance. Dance give warriors courage for fight. Do not leave." Lalawethika's strong voice and stronger grip per-suaded Peter to stay and endure what looked like a festival to death.

The next morning two parties of warriors, painted in red and black and wearing feathers in their hair, rode out screaming their war cry at the top of their lungs. Families and friends stood by and yelled with them until they were out of sight, then everyone silently went back to their chores, or sat in the sun discussing what would happen to the white settlers.

Peter took a long walk along the river, away from the village.

Chapter XXIII

Nuttak made no concession to the fact that her baby was due soon. She went about her normal daily routine even though a few women told her she may have two babies inside her. She only smiled at the thought, but would leave that up to the Great Spirit.

"Wematin, go away. You not help by sitting here. I have many days before my time comes. Even then you be no help. This women do. I will go to the birth lodge when it is time. So go hunt. Your friends say you still have much to learn. Have you forgotten the cat and the bear? Do something useful. Bring home meat."

"Are ya banishin' me from the house? You don't want me around?"

Nuttak put her hands on her hips and frowned at him. "Do white men hang around their wives when they give birth?"

"Well, yes, if they're needed."

"White woman very weak if she need man to help her give birth."

Peter opened his mouth to say something in defense of white men and women, but decided it was a losing battle. Nuttak would have her way as she always did, so with a heavy heart he picked up his bow, quiver, and pouch of pemmican. "Very well, stubborn woman, I will go hunting. I might be gone three days." He put his arms around her and kissed her. "Maybe the next time I kiss you I will also kiss the head of a little babe." He smiled a very weak smile and walked to the door.

He knew he would not stay away so long if he could help it. He put a hand on her father's shoulder and went to gather his friends.

"So, Nuttak kick you out of house," Gray Wolf smiled when Peter approached. "You come with us now?"

"Yes, I come with you. She doesn't want me around."

"What we tell you? It is way with women. Better to hunt than watch woman."

"Yes. I reckon you're right." Peter and the same four young men he had hunted with during the winter headed west. Hunting would be better in that direction. There were more villages to the south and east. Travel to the north would take them into Iroquois country and the French fort, so west it was. Peter had spent five winter months in the west. Even with the new growth and the greening of the trees he recognized many landmarks.

"Wematin, you look for trail. We see if you got good eyes." Peter stared at Gray Wolf. This was the first time he had been ask to lead a hunt, but he stuck out his chest and nodded proudly.

The hunting party was out for five days, and four of them had a deer to carry. One doe was seen nursing its fawn and the men smiled to themselves. "Not kill doe. Little one need milk to grow. We wait." It was nearly dark when the doe was spotted and they were on their way home. They continued walking, watching for wolves or bears that might take their kills. By midmorning of the sixth day the five men returned to the village.

"Nuttak?" Peter called expecting her to poke her head out of the flap. "Nuttak?" Peter entered the wigwam, but the fire circle was cold and her father lay on his bench covered with blankets.

"Father?" Peter approached the old man. It was easier to call him father rather than use his name, Lalawethika. "What is the matter? Are you sick?"

"I die tomorrow."

"No you won't. You were well when I left six days ago."

"I have fever. I die tomorrow. Carry me from village. Let me die by river. It talk to me when it go over rocks. Promise me, Wematin. You must not let me die inside. It is very bad medicine to die inside. I must die in the open air where the sky father can find me." Lalawethika's voice grew weaker as he spoke and he looked imploringly into Peter's eyes.

"Okay. I will do as you wish. But, first tell me where is Nuttak?"

"Nuttak go to my sister. Across river. She must not stay here. Maybe she have fever. I not know. Now, carry me. I too weak to walk so far."

"Now? You want me to carry you now?" Peter was unable to think straight. He kept repeating what Lalawethika said as he tried to understand. His meaning was not penetrating.

"Now. I grow too weak to talk."

Peter continued to stare at the old man, knowing he was not old enough to die, and was well enough when he left to go hunting.

"I will get you some corncakes to keep so you will not go hungry." Peter wrapped the buffalo blanket around the old man and picked him up."You don't weigh as much as the deer I shot on the hunt." A very small smile appeared on the old man's lips as Peter carried him out into the sunshine. He closed his eyes. The inside of the wigwam had been quite dark with no fire.

People watched as Peter carried Lalawethika toward the river. No one approached and no one spoke. They understood why he was wrapped in a blanket when the sun had warmed the air and small children were running around without clothing. Peter looked neither to the right nor left but straight ahead, turned left when he reached the river and walked a hundred yards before finding the rocks in the water that Lalawethika had alluded to.

"We are here, father. I will lay you on the soft grass, and place moss under your head so you may see the river."

"You good man, Wematin. I glad you are Nuttak's husband. Now, when she returns to the house you will have child, maybe a son like you." Peter nodded and finished making a pillow of moss for the old man's head, and stood up.

"I will come back tonight to see if you want anything." Lalawethika smiled and closed his eyes. Peter looked at the river. "It's a nice place to be."

"It is good place to die," whispered Lalawethika.

Peter hurried to Red Bird and asked her for some corncakes to take to Lalawethika. "He says he is going to die tomorrow."

"He is sick. Maybe corncakes make him feel better, but if he say he die, he will die."

"But, he's not old enough to die."

Red Bird looked at him and silently handed him a small pouch with two corncakes. She turned and re-entered the wigwam. Peter hurried back to where he left Lalawethika and laid the pouch on his stomach where he could easily reach it. Lalawethika looked like he was asleep, but when Peter looked more closely he could see his eyelids move. He breathed a sigh of relief and left him alone.

Peter was eager to know where Nuttak was so he wadded across the creek at the usual wading place. This was a place where the people had placed many large rocks for walking on but far enough apart so the water could flow around them. It was a shallow creek that flowed into the river next to the village, and in the summer people walked through the water in bare feet. Peter chose to use the rocks rather than get his moccasins wet.

"Have you seen Nuttak?" he asked of the first woman he saw.

"Nuttak in birthing lodge. You stay away. No men go there, she said forcefully." Peter had heard his wife tell him this so many times he could hear her voice repeat it now.

"But I want to know she's okay?" The woman laughed at him and turned away. Peter brushed his hand across his eyes to clear away the tears that were clouding his vision. He waded back across the creek and went to Askuwheteau's house.

Fortunately, the chief was sitting outside where he watched his two boys wrestle each other. The older boy, Black Hawk, would be leaving soon to live with an uncle across the creek. His younger brother, Eagle Feather would have to wait two more years.

"Askuwheteau. I am glad to see you."

"You went on hunting trip and Nuttak went to birthing lodge."

"If you know that, then you must know that her father says he is dying and I had to take him outside."

"Red Bird told me you came for corncakes to feed him. I did not know he was sick. I will go to him so I can say goodbye. He was good friend." He didn't move, but continued to smoke his pipe.

"I have come to ask you a question. I am worried about Nuttak, but the women will not let me see her."

"No, you cannot. I will ask Red Bird to find out. You come back tomorrow. I tell you what I know." Askuwheteau looked at Peter sympathetically.

"Thank you, brother. I will come back tomorrow." He left and walked along the river, not knowing what else to do with himself.

When he woke up the next morning, Peter rushed over to see Red Bird. "What have you learned. Is Nuttak okay?"

"She okay. She resting in birthing lodge."

"Why can't she have the baby at home?"

"No. Never. We once went into forest to be alone in little hut we make. We stay for one moon, then bring baby home. French make us build special lodge for birthing. We not always alone. Other women bring food. I take food to Nuttak. You brother. Now, she sister."

"No. I could not wait a full moon to find out if she and the baby are okay."

Askuwheteau laughed and slapped a hand on his leg. "You not understand. Do not speak of this. Nuttak be okay. Red Bird help."

"I guess that will have to do. Thank you Askuwheteau, my brother." Peter put his hand on the chief's arm and looked into his eyes. "Thank you."

"You go home now."

Peter went back to the wigwam he had shared with Nuttak and her father, but he couldn't rest. He got up and grabbed his bow and arrow. It was growing dark, but he went into the woods and then walked the trail he often walked when he needed to be alone to think. He came to the spot where he left Lalawethika on his blanket. "How are you feeling, father?"

"I die soon. You go now. Leave me in peace."

Peter put a hand on top of Lalawethika's boney hand and said goodbye. He stood up and walked away looking down at the ground in front of him. *What will I do without him? He is wise and has been so good to me. He is not so old but he has seen much. I would have liked to hear more from him. Now I never will.* Peter stopped and turned to look back at the old man, now bathed in moonlight. He listened as the water washed over the rocks in the river making a soothing, bubbling sound. An owl hooted somewhere in the forest.

Chapter XXIV

Peter's mind was not on hunting. He only wanted to walk and think, but a good hunter does not allow his mind to wander from the task at hand. Squirrels had returned to their nests for the night, and the only sound he heard was his own footsteps. Not even a breeze stirred the leaves in the trees. The trail he followed ran along the edge of the creek. He was suddenly startled to see two does with their fawns grazing. Peter stood still. *Such a beautiful sight.* He stood quietly watching them as they stood in full moonlight. *I haven't the heart to kill a single one of 'em. Any one family in the village could certainly use the meat, but I haven't the heart. Those little fawns are too young to lose their mothers. Not today.* Peter kept watch as the four animals shook their short white tails. The does looked up and stared straight at Peter with no fear in their eyes, only curiosity. Then they all moved slowly into the forest and disappeared.

After some walking, Peter grew tired and lay down under a large oak tree with his bow and arrows on the ground beside him. Before he knew it he awoke with the sun in his eyes. "Blarney. I fell asleep. Lalawethika. Nuttak. I must see to them." He got up and hurried back along the trail to the spot where he left his father-in-law. "Lalawethika? Are you there?" The old man's face was gray, and when Peter touched him, the skin was cold. "Oh, father. How did you know with such certainty?" Peter pulled the robe over the old man's face and trotted into the village and straight for Askuwheteau's wigwam.

"Brother. Askuwheteau. I must speak with you." He sounded agitated.

Askuwheteau looked at the pain in Peter's eyes and spoke calmly, "you want to know what to do with Lalawethika's body. I will help you." He rose from where he had been sitting outside his wigwam. "We will carry him to the burial ground. Others will help us. It is sad that Nuttak knows nothing of this. My wife will tell her later, after baby is born."

"Thank you, brother. I am grateful to you." Askuwheteau told his wife where he was going, and the two of them walked to the place where Peter left Lalawethika. They wrapped the body in a wool blanket and laid him on his buffalo robe. "He is not heavy. I will carry him."

"Follow me." Peter followed Askuwheteau and the two friends. As they passed within site of the village other people began to follow. The burial grounds covered a rather large area of perhaps an acre. Many sticks protruded from the ground with feathers and beads decorating them. "We place him here. Room for many more." Askuwheteau stopped and pointed to a spot of smooth earth. One of the friends put a pole into the ground and began to dig a hole about eighteen inches deep. Another pole was placed in the ground at what would be the foot. "His head must face place where sun sets."

Women began to appear and helped to collect stones to line the bottom of the grave. Once Lalawethika's body was placed in the hole the blanket was pulled aside and his bow and quiver were placed in his right hand. His sacred pipe was placed near his left hand, along with a pouch of tobacco. "These things he will need in next world." Askuwheteau told Peter.

Food was added next. "He had no wife to sing for him. My wife and her sisters will sing and dance." The ceremony continued for the rest of the day and when everyone left to return to the village, two men remained to cover the body with dirt and pile rocks to prevent wild animals from digging it up.

That same evening Peter sat again in the empty wigwam. *Now that her father is buried, I have to find out how Nuttak is doing. Has she given birth yet? Am I a father? Do I have a son?*

Peter fell asleep waking many times to the complete silence of the village. *Damn. It be too quiet.* He rose and went outside. Above, a full spring moon gave the village an eerie incandescence. The bark covering on the wigwams emitted a silvery gleam. He sat down and stared up at the sky. "You moon; you shine on everything I hold dear. If only you could tell the answer to my questions." As Peter spoke in a soft voice an old shaggy dog lumbered up to him and lay down on the hard packed earth for comfort. "Old dog, where did you come from?" Peter scratched the dog's head and behind the ears, to the dog's obvious pleasure. Neither one made a sound, but the dog's tail wagged so strongly it made a womp womp sound as it hit the ground. "Come, you can keep me company tonight." He pulled back the flap over the door opening and the two of them went inside. The dog curled up near the small fire in the center of the room and Peter crawled under his wool blanket and finally slept.

Chapter XXV

A few days went by with no word about Nuttak. Peter didn't dare leave the village. He ate with Askuwheteau so he saw Red Bird each day. She went across the creek to the birthing lodge, but only asked quietly so as not to annoy Nuttak. Each night Peter returned to the empty wigwam and his blankets with an increasingly worried mind and heavy heart. He was helpless.

Sunlight on the lids of Peter's eyes woke him. The flap on the door had been pulled aside. "Who is it?" The figure standing there was silhouetted against the bright morning light.

"Wematin. Come outside. I talk to you." The voice was that of Askuwheteau's wife, Red Bird.

Peter threw off the blanket and hurried outside in his bare feet accidentally kicking the dog that had adopted him as he went. "What is it? Is the baby born? Is Nuttak okay? When can I see them?"

"Slow down. You hurry too much. I not speak so good." She looked at him angrily, but almost as quickly her expression turned to one of concern. "I speak about Nuttak, but it is not good. Nuttak dead. Baby dead. Baby too big for little body."

Peter fell to his knees. His whaling brought out his neighbors to see what had caused such a cry. Peter didn't care that all Indian men were trained at birth to be tough and not cry. "Wematin, stop this noise. It is not right."

"I don't care. I loved her and now because of me she's gone." He rocked back and forth on his knees. "I want to see her. I want to see her now. Take me to her."

"She be brought to you very soon. We go with you to the burial ground." When Red Bird finished speaking she turned and walked away. His neighbors went back to their homes, and Peter went inside and threw himself down onto his blankets and cried like he had not cried since being a child. Great sobs came from his throat and he didn't care who heard. He stopped caring about anything. He only wanted Nuttak to come back to him. Nothing else mattered. Nothing.

Nuttak's body was brought to him a few hours later. Her cousins and friends had dressed her in a beautiful soft deer hide, decorated with colorful beads. A band was put around her head and her hair was combed and placed on her shoulders. A silver amulet was on each arm and a silver necklace hung from her neck. Her moccasins were also decorated with beads. She had been placed on a large piece of bark that served as a litter. Peter knelt on the ground and kissed her lips. "My sweet, sweet wife. I should not a married ya. You would be alive but for me." His eyes were filled with tears and he wiped them away with the back of his hands.

Askuwheteau pulled Peter back and up onto his feet. "Not say these things," he whispered. "You made her happy. You must remember that. She goes to live with her ancestors now. We help to prepare her way. Two men go ahead, prepare burial place. Red Bird and my sons will bring feast for her journey."

Nuttak was placed in the shallow grave next to her father. Food and small tools, sewing needles and sinew were placed beside her so that she might make more clothing in the other world. Peter followed, but said nothing. *I can't go along with this.*

Each of the people at the burial site ate a few bits of food and the rest was placed in the grave. Hours later after everyone left and Peter was alone, he repeated the only prayer he knew, the Lord's Prayer. Then he lay on the ground next to the mound of dirt and rocks that covered her and wept. Peter was left alone to grieve. He stayed by her side and later that night he fell asleep. He didn't wake until morning when the dog licked his face. He stood up and looked one last time at her grave.

Chapter XXVI

Peter didn't know what to do with himself. Askuwheteau invited him to return to his wigwam where he could eat and sleep. Red Bird said she would rather he stayed with them like he had before marrying Nuttak. That wigwam would be given to another family. Peter agreed. The wigwam held too many memories.

A few days later Peter went to his friends, White Antelope and Gray Wolf. "Come, let us hunt. I need to be doing something useful."

"This is good. This hanging of head not good. Let us hunt. We kill deer today, maybe bear." White Antelope put his hand on Peter's shoulder and gave it a gentle squeeze.

"Yes, we kill a bear today." Spring had arrived, and if he had been paying attention he would have noticed that the trees were turning more green.

"Some bear may be out with cubs. We will see. I know bear den." White Antelope led them another mile when they all stopped suddenly and stared. Ahead of them in the middle of the trail was a small bear cub. "Mother near." White Antelope turned, looking behind them and said in a quiet voice, "Bear."

Peter and Gray Wolf turned to see the mother bear standing up on her hind legs. At the same moment she let loose a deafening roar. Gray Wolf had the only rifle among the three and he fired, hitting the bear in the chest. A moment later Peter and White Antelope let loose their arrows. With no time to place another arrow, they dropped them and grabbed their tomahawks, poised to defend themselves. The bear dropped to all fours and ran toward them, but just as the three men were about to hit her with their tomahawks the mother bear fell at their feet. A few blows with a tomahawk assured them that she was dead.

Behind them they could hear the cub crying, and without another thought Gray Wolf turned and shot the cub, killing it instantly.

"Poor little cub. He had no mother to care for him," whispered Peter.

"You sound like woman, Wematin. My wife like having soft cub fur."

"Yes, of course," Peter answered, quickly recovering from the revulsion he felt at killing a baby animal. He would have preferred to let it grow up, but he also realized it was too young to survive on its own.

When the three returned to the village Peter carried his share of the meat to Askuwheteau's wigwam and handed it to Red Bird.

She smiled. "You are good hunter, Wematin. Come, sit.

Peter joined other hunting parties and for the next two months worked hard to bring meat to the village. Then in early June he was asked to join a different party.

"Wematin." Askuwheteau called Peter out of a deep sleep. "Come out."

"What's wrong?" Peter didn't bother to put on a shirt or moccasins and staggered out as he rubbed his eyes. "Has something happened?"

"Nothing wrong. I like to be outside where air is clean."

"You woke me up to tell me that?"

"No, my brother," Askuwheteau laughed. "You go on journey. A long journey."

"A journey? Where?" Peter did not want to go on a warring trip, and Askuwheteau did not need to tell him to hunt. He had been hunting almost every day for many weeks.

"You go on trading trip. We have many furs from winter. We trade for gun powder, rifles, blankets and other things. Go talk to Sound Of Thunder. He will tell you what you need to know. You find him in council house."

"Thank you, brother. I will go and talk with Sound Of Thunder now." They each put a hand on the other's shoulder and Peter went inside to get his moccasins. It was now late spring and the past week had been hot so he needed nothing more than his breech cloth as did many of the other men.

"Sound Of Thunder, I have come to help you. I am honored to join you on this journey but Askuwheteau did not tell me where." Peter stood before the tall strong man who had been a teacher and a friend.

"Askuwheteau speaks well of you. He told me you should be on this trip. We put furs here where they be safe. We go by canoe to Niagara where we trade for blankets, powder and shot. Many things we need." Sound of Thunder pointed to the piles of furs stacked at the far end of the council house.

"Yes, I have brought many here this past winter." He looked at the pile and knew they would be worth a lot in trade. The village would receive a lot in return, and as the village grew many more blankets would be needed.

"Askuwheteau says you okay hunter. Bring many furs."

Peter smiled at the older man standing before him, a man whose age Peter was never able to determinate, but a man whose strong arms were decorated with silver amulets and many scars. One raw looking scar ran from his forehead to his chin barely missing his left eye. Peter thought to himself, *This man has been in some pretty tough fights.*

The two men worked diligently the rest of the day, carrying armloads of furs to the six canoes. Each had room for the rowers to stow rifles, bow and arrows, tomahawks and dried foods. Then on the third morning Peter bid farewell to Askuwheteau. "Sound of Thunder says that if all goes according to plan we should return in about three or four weeks." His sons ran down to the river to see Peter leave. "You are brave little warriors. Be strong and make your father proud." They both beamed their smiles at Peter.

"May Great Spirit make you good journey." The two put a hand on each other's shoulders, and Peter thought he saw a sadness in the man's eyes he had not seen before. Peter joined the eleven other men in the canoes.

"Askuwheteau. Who will hunt for you while I am away?"

"You not only hunter in village. We not go hungry. We have food of forest and fields, and dried meat you brought to us." With that Askuwheteau laughed out loud showing his few missing teeth.

Askuwheteau watched Peter until he was out of sight, then he walked back to his wigwam as his sons ran ahead of him. Red Bird watched and spoke to him in Shawnee. "Why you hang your head? You are chief. You do not hang head." She stopped just short of scolding the chief.

"Leave me alone, woman. I have heavy heart today."

She looked at him closely. "You think Wematin will not return?"

"I have given him chance to leave us if he wants."

"Why? He your brother now."

"He has been very sad after Nuttak die. I think he will never be happy again if he stays with us. It will be his choice. He must decide what he wants to do. I only give him the chance to decide."

The first day on the lake Peter found he was using muscles he had never used before. He had never rowed a canoe and was having to learn fast. "You row like squaw, Wematin." His canoe mate, Keme, laughed at him. The result was that they fell behind the others. That night when they stopped to camp, Keme told the others. "Wematin row like squaw." The others laughed, but Peter remained silent. He knew the teasing was all in good fun.

"I've never done this before. Give me time. I will learn and be as good as you." Everyone laughed again. *What a braggart I am. My muscles are strong from the bow, but ache like the devil from rowing. And these blisters on my hands will probably bleed tomorrow.*

By mid morning of the second day a rain storm blew in from the southwest, whipping up strong waves that blew the canoes further north toward the center of the lake. "We must keep the land in sight." Kitchi yelled in Shawnee to the men in the other canoes. He had been to Niagara before, on other fur trading trips, and was the guide on this one.

Peter rowed as hard as he could to keep the shore in sight. *My arms feel like they will break off from so much hard rowing.* To Keme he yelled over the sound of the rain and wind, "Keme. Wouldn't we be better off rowing closer to the shore?"

"Kitchi say too much tree limb in water. Break canoe."

"Damn. Just my luck." He looked longingly toward the shore.

"Those trees might break the wind. Out here we have nothing to stop it or even slow it down."

Kitchi yelled again. "Stay close to other canoe. Wematin, you work harder. I know safe place to put canoes." He continued to row east as the wind continued to blow from the southwest. The direction of the wind was a help as well as a curse. It blew them east, but they had to fight to keep it from blowing them north across the lake.

"Where is this safe place?" Peter yelled.

"You be patient, Wematin."

"Easy for you to say," Peter muttered to himself.

They beached the canoes that night and endured a cold and wet camp. By morning the storm had passed and the sun rose into a cloudless sky. As they traveled the sun dried and warmed them.

Three days later they arrived at Niagara and pulled out southwest of the great falls on the Niagara River.

"Wematin, help to carry furs to trading post."

"Where is it? I don't see anything but wigwams and tents."

"Up hill, behind trees."

Peter grabbed a load and carried it on his back. "I still don't see it." They followed a well worn trail from the river through the scattered wigwams, tents and trees. A few wooden houses and log cabins were scattered along the trail. "Short walk? My legs are weak from sitting in that canoe for five days." With each of the twelve men carrying a load all the furs were quickly delivered to the trading post.

"Wematin." Keme dropped his last load of furs. Together the men went back to their canoes and retrieved their rifles, bows and arrows. The canoes were secured among fallen trees and cattails that grew along the river's edge. They left the counting and negotiating to Kitchi. "Come, I show you something."

Peter followed Keme for about four miles upriver. "I hear a waterfall. Sounds like a pretty big one."

"You never see like this one." Keme smiled as they continued to walk.

The roar grew louder. Another two miles and Peter looked at the river that was suddenly far below. "What is that? It looks like a low cloud in the river."

"That is water from falls."

"Wow! What a sight. That has to be the biggest falls in the world."

"You like?" Keme smiled as he looked at the surprise on Peter's face.

"Who wouldn't like this? This is wonderful." The two of them sat down and watched the falls until the sun moved low in the west. "Keme, look. The colors in the spray."

"Sun make pretty colors." Together they sat until almost dark.

Chapter XXVII

"I go find food. You come?" Keme stood up and stretched his arms into the air.

"I want to sit here a little longer. I will join you later." Peter looked at the falls and didn't turn around. "I may never get to see this again. We should have a good moon tonight and I want to see how it looks then." He sat and stared at the falls. The setting sun created a rainbow.

"Hello. Are you an Indian?" A voice sounding distinctly like that of a white man startled Peter. He turned and stared at a white man with light brown hair, dressed as an Iroquois.

"Who are you? I didn't hear you walk up."

"You don't sound like an Indian either." The man came closer and sat down next to Peter.

"Neither do you and you sure don't look like one. I'm Peter Looney from Virginia."

"William Phillips of New York[5]. Are you alone?" Phillips held out his hand to Peter.

"At the moment I am. I came here with a party from Detroit to trade furs. The others are about four miles downriver."

"How did you get to Detroit if your home is in Virginia?"

"I was captured a year ago, though in some ways it seems like a lifetime ago. It feels kinda strange to hear well spoken English. I've lived as a Shawnee for the past year."

"I was captured at Oswego. The French battered the fort to pieces and the Indians went on a killing spree inside the fort. I was lucky to survive, only to be captured."

"When was that?"

"August fourteenth of last year. The Indians would have killed everyone in the fort but the French commander, Montcalm would have none of it. He had to promise the chiefs ten thousand livres' worth of gifts from King Louis. It was a blood bath. I had nightmares for months afterward."

"How were you treated?" Peter asked.

"Ha." He laughed sarcastically. "Like a slave. I walked away today. I have a wife back home and I don't even know if she still lives."

"We should return to camp. There are so many tents mixed among the wigwams, surely there are many white people there."

"Yes, but they are all French."

"Do you speak French?"

"No, but I can understand a few words." They stood up and began the four mile walk back to the camp.

"Do you carry any food with you?" William asked.

"I have only a little dried pemmican in my pouch. We can find food in the camp."

"You must be quiet and speak only Shawnee. As for me I must be very careful. I don't dare be seen by anyone I know. I'm afraid they will turn me over to the Iroquois. If they do I would surely be killed."

Hours later the two of them had filled their hands with much of the food that had been set out for the traders, and then quietly melted into the darkness surrounding the camp. With so many people, both Indian and white milling around in the camp it seemed that no one took notice of them.

As they walked away Phillips asked, "Did you hear the two French commanders talking to the trader?"

"Yes, but I don't understand French."

"They said a party of two hundred-eighty French soldiers had arrived downriver from Catarequi.[6]"

"Where's that?" Peter had finished the turkey leg and thigh and was licking his fingers.

"It's about 1400 miles away, on the northeast part of Lake Ontario. That's the lake just north of where we are now. They are on their way to Fort Duquesne."

"That's not good, not good at all."

"Why so?"

"A large party of Shawnee left about six weeks ago for Fort Duquesne to fight the English."

"Sounds like another battle."

"I fear so, and I want no part of it."

"Nor I. I suggest we get out of here before they leave in the morning." Phillips looked at Peter. All he could see were the whites of his eyes

Peter hesitated. "I should go with you. But, I have many new friends among the Shawnee. I have an adopted brother who has been more like an uncle than a brother. This will sadden him."

"But think of your white family. You've been gone for over a year and they don't even know if you're alive or not. You must remember your own kind."

"Yes. I suppose you're right." Peter felt a tightening in his chest, over his heart. He knew that if he left he was leaving another life behind him. Whatever he decided it would be a life without Nuttak. "I'll go."

Chapter XXVIII

Peter woke before dawn listening to the birds in the trees overhead, and he poked William Phillips to wake up. Silently, they crept out of their woodland hiding place. The camp was many miles behind them but fear that some of the Indians may have wanted to follow them made them cautious. The previous evening they had used the light from the waning moon and walked away from the trading post with its camp of wigwams, tents, hundreds of French soldiers and an unknown number of Indians.

"You realize we have no idea how far we'll have to walk. I do have my bow and arrows. Lucky for me I carried them with me when Keme took me off to see the falls."

"Even if you find something to shoot we don't dare light a fire."

Peter contemplated this problem for a moment. "Well, I'll share what little pemmican I have here in my pouch. Maybe by tomorrow we'll be far enough away to build a small fire to roast a turkey or a rabbit." The thought of soft rabbit fur gave a quick stab to his heart. Nuttak had made a small blanket of rabbit furs for the baby that never was.

Peter looked at the man, barely making him out in the predawn darkness. "You will have to lead. I've never been in this country before, William, or can I call you Will."

"It's good to hear the sound of the English language again. Call me Will, if you like."

"My Shawnee name is Wematin but call me Peter."

"You asked if I was familiar with this country. I am somewhat. Oswego is on the lake further northeast. We can't go there, though. It was burned to the ground. We can't go to Fort Ontario either. The British destroyed it in order to better supply Fort Oswego. What a pest hole that was. More men died of disease than bullets. Getting past this swampy land will be our first concern. There could be snakes in these waters, so be careful."

"Water moccasins are poisonous. I sure wouldn't want to spend a year living with the Shawnee just to die here of a snake bite." Peter looked at the sky. "The sun should be up in another hour." After hearing William mention snakes, he began to look more carefully where he stepped.

"Use a stick to stir up the water. It may chase them away and make the way clear for us."

That night brought them to a spot of solid ground. Peter shot no food, mainly because he never saw anything to shoot. Without a fire he wouldn't be able to cook it anyway, so they bedded as best they could. William woke first as the sky turned light enough for them to see. "Peter, wake up."

"Nuttak?" Peter rolled over but found himself face to face with a rabbit. "Ah, you little varmint. You'd be a tasty one now." He no sooner spoke than the rabbit hopped away.

"Who's Nuttak?"

"What?" Peter sat up and rubbed his eyes. His stomach growled. "It's somebody I knew." Talking about Nuttak would have been painful. He preferred to keep that subject private. It was bad enough that he thought of her daily, and hiking through swamp land dressed like an Indian didn't make it any easier.

"I can hear your stomach growl. Mine has been doing the same."

As Peter stretched his arms and legs he looked around at the landscape before him. "Maybe tonight we can dare light a fire." He checked the soles of his moccasins. "I will need to put some bark inside my moccasins. They are showing a lot o' wear. This swampy land is no help either."

"I'd better do the same." One tool both men had with them was a hunting knife. With that they made a quick and temporary repair, and continued walking.

"How long do you reckon before we meet better country?" Peter's only reference was the trip across the Shenandoah Mountains to the Ohio and beyond.

"The Mohawk River is one-hundred-forty miles 'til it reaches the Hudson River."

"So, we'd better start paying attention to where the game be, or we'll starve to death and me with a bow and arrows. That be a disgrace I don't care to endure."

The two men walked another day before reaching the headwaters of the Mohawk River. "We best stay on the southern side, if you don't want to do a lot of swimming." William began to cross over. The headwaters in the middle of summer was little more than a few scattered mud puddles.

"Are ya tellin' me the river grows bigger as we follow along?"

"I am. You'll see. Even in summer it will be wide though not too much trouble. From fall to spring it will be a raging torrent tearing up everything in its path."

Peter kept his bow at the ready hoping to spot something they could cook, but William had a tendency to talk and his voice carried further than was good for their stomachs. Peter frequently held his fingers to his mouth in an effort to quiet him, but it never lasted long enough.

That night Peter tried to explain to William the importance of quiet in the woods. "Did you not know that a deer can hear ya comin' for a mile before you ever see it? Likewise, every animal in the forest can smell ya too."

"I'm sorry, Peter. I'm no hunter. Never was. I was a carpenter like my father."

"Please try, William. Our lives depend on our ability to hunt food. If it be over one hundred miles, do ya know how long it will take us to reach the confluence? I reckon on ten to fourteen days, depending on how many miles we can cover each day."

"I know you're right, Peter. We must find something to eat." The next day Peter woke up early and William was quiet as they carefully

144

made their way along the river. He spotted a deer, but it was too quick. An hour before dusk he spotted a turkey and the two men ate their fill next to a warm fire.

The turkey didn't last long. They ate the rest for breakfast and trudged on for another two days. Peter kept watch over William knowing his backwoods experience was nil. By the morning of the third day William was slowing down. "I'm not sure how long I can walk without food. Can't you use that bow and arrow and shoot something?"

"Here, eat this." He handed William the last piece of pemmican from his pouch. "Keep quiet and walk softly. Keep your eyes open for something we can cook." Peter took an arrow and placed it on the bow holding it gently with his left finger and with his right thumb and forefinger on the notched end of the arrow.

The promise of hot food quieted William and he made no more complaints. Both of them walked more slowly in hopes of finding some small game they could cook. It was mid afternoon when William complained of being weak. They walked for another few hours looking and watching.

William was just about to issue a complaint when Peter held up his left hand and signaled for William to get down, then Peter crouched on his left knee and pulled back slowly on the bow string. William was looking around, bobbing his head as he did so when he heard the arrow singing through the trees.

"Got him."

"Got what? I didn't see anything."

"We'll have turkey for dinner tonight." Peter stood up and ran ahead to where the turkey lay on a bed of pine needles and dry leaves. But, for Peter's sharp eye he would never have seen the turkey, it blended so well with the underbrush and dead leaves.

"Can we stop now, Peter and cook it? I'm nearly starved."

"We'll stop shortly. Best to cook it and be done with it before dark. The fire will be too easy to spot in this open country."

"I'm not sure how much longer I can wait."

"Patience, William. Going without will be good training for what may be leaner days ahead. I'm a stranger in this country so I don't know what be ahead of us."

As they waited for the turkey to cook over a small fire William began asking questions. "So, you made friends with those Indians?"

"Well, yes. I thought I's be there for a long time. One of the chiefs adopted me as his brother."

"And he let you come on a trading trip?"

"He asked me to come."

"I'll bet he knew you would leave if you had a chance."

"Why would he do that?"

"Only you can answer that, Peter."

Three more days and William began talking about food again. "I'd sure like a corn cake right about now; a nice crisp corn cake with a heaping of butter. I can almost taste it."

"Stop it, William. You're only makin' things worse for yourself."

"I can't help it. I'm going to starve out here if we don't find food again soon. I couldn't sleep last night from thinking about food. I'll just sit here on this old log a minute." William sat down on the nearest old tree that had been uprooted due to age and probably a lightning strike.

"Lean on me, William. We can't afford to stop." Peter put one arm around William and pulled William's arm over his shoulder. This may take us a little longer, but we gotta keep movin'."

"How can you keep going? What drives you, Peter?"

"I learned on many hunting trips to go for days without food. I reckon it's something you have to learn. The Shawnee children learn at an early age. They go into the forest and live for four or five days without food waiting for their spirit to find them."

"Sounds like rubbish to me." William limped along with Peter holding him up.

Suddenly Peter stopped and looked around. "I smell something. The smoke of a cooking fire. Come. Friendly or not, there be people ahead, and where there be people, there be food."

"What if they're hostiles? They might kill us?"

"There's only one way to find out." Peter pulled William along.

Chapter XXIX

Two barking dogs appeared from behind brush and a thick stand of trees. They stopped in front of Peter and William, blocking their way. The dogs continued to bark as if telling them to go no further. Presently three Indians arrived on horseback. Then the dogs stood still with their tongues hanging out and their tails wagging.

"They look like Mohawks." William observed and collapsed onto the ground at Peter's feet. Peter looked at the three men. Using hand signals he indicated their need for food.

"You are dressed like Shawnee, and that man dressed like Iroquois. Why?" One of the two men asked Peter in English.

Peter pointed to himself. "I am Peter Looney. I was captured in Virginia by the Shawnee one year ago. I left them and wish to return home. My friend here has also escaped capture and is going home."

"We do not want to keep you. Come and rest today. We will give you food. You have far to go."

"You are very kind. You also speak very good English."

"We are friends of the English."

Peter looked at William then back at the man and smiled, nodding his head. "It's good to be among English friends."

Peter and William rested in the shade of several old oak trees that stood next to the little creek that fed into the Mohawk River. William ate the small amount of food given them and fell asleep. Peter relished the cooked venison as much as William, but his restlessness led him down the creek to gaze across the Mohawk River. Near his feet he could see fish swimming peacefully. *So many things remind me of Nuttak*, and turned around to lie down and nap next to William and look up at the thick limbs of the oak trees. "It be good to rest a bit."

The Mohawks wanted to trade, so Peter traded his bow and arrows for new moccasins for both him and William.

During their two days with the Mohawks Peter and William learned a little more of the war between the white Americans and the French. In turn they told of their experiences with the Shawnee and Iroquois.

On the third day they left and walked for several hours before William broke the silence. "I'm sorry about your Indian squaw, but I understand your attachment to the people."

"I told that chief my story, but I'd not like to say any more on the subject." Peter spoke softly but in a tone of voice that made the hair on William's neck stand up.

"I understand. Not another word." In an attempt to change the subject but keep talking he continued, "It does feel good to have new moccasins and a full stomach."

"Yes. I agree." Peter didn't care to talk. His mind was filled with memories.

"Another two days and we can stop at William Johnson's place. He might give us food."

"Is this a friend of yours?"

"He is a friend of the Three Nations, and a powerful and important Indian agent. The Iroquois adopted him and he speaks for them. He was treated far better than I was. He's also very rich. He made his money as an Indian trader. The Indians have much respect for him because he treats them fairly, and he fights with the bureaucrats on their behalf. This place where we're going is next to his trading post. If he's not at home, we might be able to get something from the trading post."

"Do you really think he will help us?"

"I hope so. We have to cross the river to where his house stands."

Peter looked at the woods that lined the river bank, "I don't see a house." William kept walking.

"We'll cross here. It's not so deep, but we'll still have to swim part of the way. I hope you can swim."

"Aye. Me brothers made me learn when I was barely able to walk."

By the time they approached Johnson's house their moccasins and breech clothes had dried. They knocked on the large heavy front door. A young woman answered and looked them up and down.

"Why are you dressed as Indians? I can tell the difference, you know."

William spoke first. "We're sorry to bother you, Ma'am. Is Mr. Johnson at home?"

"No. Sir Johnson has gone to Albany on business. What is it you want with him?"

Peter stepped forward. "We don't mean to bother you ma'am, but we are in need of something to eat and wondered if Mr. Johnson could help us."

"First, tell me why two white men, dressed as Indians, would be in need of food."

"Well, ma'am. You see, it's like this. We were captives of the Indians and just escaped about a week ago. We're tryin' to get back to our homes."

"I see. Wait here and I'll see what I can do."

"Yes, ma'am." Peter stood back as the door closed. He and William sat down on the front steps to wait.

The girl that opened the door reminded Peter of Nuttak. She was an attractive, young Indian squaw but he didn't know what tribe. Her dress and hair ornaments were different, but he barely noticed as he focused on her dark eyes and full lips. He realized he had told her they had been captured by Indians and worried as to what she might make of that information. He noted that she spoke English as well as William.

Peter looked at the large brick house. "I ain't never seen a house this big, and all in brick, with fancy windows. He must have a very big family to have such a big house."

"I don't know anything about that. I only know what I hear or read in the papers," remarked William.

A few minutes later the girl returned with a cloth tied up at its corners. "I've put in some bread that was baked this morning, a little cheese and cold, cooked beef left over from yesterday. There are also a few pears. I hope that will do. Good luck to you in returning to your homes."

"You are most kind. Thank you very much." They both stood up, William took the food as the girl closed the door.

William and Peter walked back towards the river. "Well, we will not starve today or tomorrow. This sack feels heavy enough to feed us for two or three days."

"There be more roads and farms in this part of the country. So I reckon they be neighbors of this Sir Johnson. Just how does a man get to be a Sir anyway?"

"It's an honorary title bestowed on him by the British. I think they have to have the King's okay. Couldn't tell you exactly. I never met a Sir, or an Earl or any of those that have such titles. My family is all farmers and tradesmen. My father is a carpenter."

"And mine are all farmers. That little cove up ahead with the trees half bent into the river looks like a likely spot to spend the night."

Two nights later the food was gone again. Farms and houses that stood close to the river grew more numerous, and without his bow and arrows Peter couldn't hunt for food. A road ran on one side of the farms and the river on the other effectively blocking their access to water. The greater population made Peter feel hemmed in. "There be too many people around for my likin'."

"We're getting closer to Albany. You'll see many more people the further you go."

"Will it be this way all the way to Virginia, do you think?" Being dressed as an Indian also made Peter uncomfortable. "What if somebody shoots me because I look like an Indian?"

"You're unarmed, Peter. Nobody is going to shoot an unarmed man, Indian or white."

Then William turned to Peter. "About a mile ahead is the confluence of the Mohawk and the Hudson Rivers. I will have to leave you there, Peter. My home is on the upper part of the Hudson, about forty miles north of Albany."

"I'll be sorry to see ya leave, William. It's been good to have someone to travel with."

"You'll want to cross the river here to reach the other side before you get to the Hudson. It's even bigger than this river."

"Thank you, William. Goodbye and good luck to you." Peter watched as William walked away. Then he walked into the river and swam to the west side. Once there he looked back but William had disappeared.

"It be a lonely journey from now on. No one to talk to but me own self."

As Peter approached Albany he passed several more small farms with fields of corn, wheat, barley and oats. Horses and cattle were more numerous. He looked at the horses longingly. If only he could ride. Occasionally he spotted orchards but the fruit hadn't ripened yet. A few horse drawn wagons passed him along the road stirring up clouds of dust. There had been no rain in many days and the soil was dry. The fields needed rain. Some of the corn stalks were turning yellow.

He reached the town of Albany and was suddenly in the middle of a street surrounded by buildings on either side, some of them two stories high. *I ain't never seen a city before. These people be too close together.* He jumped when a carriage drawn by four horses came down the street from behind him. He ran up onto the wooden sidewalk next to an old man who was sitting on a chair outside the general store chewing tobacco and spitting onto the sidewalk.

"Hey, Injun. Where you think you're goin? Don't you know you can't walk down the middle o' the street?"

"I'm not an Indian!" Peter exclaimed. He looked at the old man with dirty pants and a grey beard several inches long. He looked annoyed at the man and kept on walking.

"Well, if you ain't a Injun, what are ya?" He called after Peter. "Whatever ya are ya still can't walk down the middle of the street. Them horses 'll just run right over ya." The man leaned forward and spit into the street, then let out a cackle of a laugh followed by intense coughing.

Peter ignored the man and continued along the sidewalk. He slowed his pace to a stroll and looked into the store windows. He paused at a dress shop which had displayed a dress with a wide flowing skirt and large puffed sleeves, all in pink satin trimmed with lace. *Now I wonder who wears such fancy stuff as that. No woman can do a decent days work in a getup like that.*

On the next block he passed a feed store where he found men loading wagons hitched to horses. "Howdy do," he said to one man who stared at him as he approached.

"Why are you dressed like an Indian? You're not an Indian."

"It's a long story." Peter kept walking until he reached the center of town. The smell of food at a hotel reminded him he hadn't eaten since two nights before. He went in and stood for a moment looking around. No one was eating, but the smell of food was strong. A few men were sitting at the tables drinking and talking. They were all laughing at something, then turned and stared at Peter. One started to rise with his fists balled up. Another man pulled him back into his chair.

Peter approached the man standing behind the bar staring at him. "Would you know where I could find work?"

"I don't hire Indians."

"I'm not an Indian. I'm Peter Looney from Virginia. I escaped from the Indians."

"Escaped? You don't say. Looks like you've been living with them for a long time."

"One year. Now, I need proper clothing and food so I can continue my way home."

"Well then. You might ask at the stables. Old man Humphrey could probably use a hand to clean out the stalls. You'll find him back of the hardware store. Next block, turn left and down the street. You can't miss it."

"Thank you." Peter nodded to the man and went back outside. He walked down the street to the hardware store and turned the corner to the stables. "Are you Mr. Humphrey?" An elderly man was sitting on a stump near the stables smoking a pipe. He looked at Peter and blew a stream of smoke into the still, hot air. With no breeze to move it, the smoke rose straight up before the man's eyes.

"No. You'll likely find Mr. Humphrey at the nearest watering hole. But, he should be back before long. If you want to wait, have a seat."

"Don't mind if I do. I been traveling for several days now."

"Where from? You don't talk like no Indian I ever met."

"My name is Peter Looney from Virginia. I'm trying to get back home. But, I need to earn enough money to buy some clothes and food."

"Well, now. Ya are in a pickle ain't ya?" The old man continued to smoke his pipe and watch the smoke rise into the air. Peter studied the man whose smoking reminded him of Askuwheteau. However, this man was dressed in wool work pants, leather shoes and a soiled white, linen shirt. His thin, white hair was tied behind with a black ribbon. On his head he wore a soiled tri-cornered, black wool hat.

After two hours of sitting, the sun dropped further into the west. The street was in complete shade. "It don't look like Mr. Humphrey be comin' back today. I'll look around for something else." Peter stood and went back to the main street. He walked another block and noticed a bar and restaurant. Oil lamps were lighting the interior making it easier to see through the window.

"Looks like I've wasted the day. Now what?" He stood outside peering in the window, breathing in the wonderful aroma of roasted beef. He took a deep breath, *I ain't smelled roasted beef in over a year now. I wonder if I got the strength to walk away.*

Peter turned to leave and accidentally walked into a man who was about to enter the bar. "Oh. Beg your pardon, Sir. Didn't mean to bump ya."

The man started to turn away, but stopped and looked at Peter. "You're a white man."

"Yes, Sir. I be Peter Looney of Augusta County, Virginia."

The man held out his hand. "My name is Lester Holston with the *London Chronicle.*[7] You look hungry, son. Come in and I'll buy you dinner." He put a hand on Peter's bare shoulder. "Never did like to eat alone. It would be nice to have someone to talk to."

"I have no money and no way to repay your generosity."

"Never mind that. You can tell me your story. I suspect a white man dressed like an Indian, and hungry to boot, probably has a story to tell. Come on." Holston took Peter by the arm and led him into a room where the warm aroma of food was almost overwhelming. His mouth watered and he almost felt faint. He let himself be led to a table.

"I ain't had nothin' to eat for the past two days."

As they waited for their food to be brought to them Holston began asking questions. "Why the Indian clothes?"

"I was captured by the Shawnee last summer and taken to one of their towns north of the Ohio." Peter answered.

Over the next hour Holston took notes as Peter told his story.

When they finished and Peter had finally eaten enough to feel full, Holston smiled. "You really were every bit as hungry as you looked, Mr. Looney. We don't see many captives coming back from the Indian camps. You're my first interview of this sort. I don't think my paper would mind if I get you dressed like a white man. Maybe cut your hair more like a white man's."

Peter put his hand to his straight, black hair that fell several inches below his shoulders. "I reckon I do look more Shawnee than white."

Peter followed Holston to the hotel he had passed earlier. They had barely crossed the lobby when the owner approached hurriedly.

"Hey. No Indians in my hotel. Mr. Holston, you know the rules."

"He's not an Indian, Mr. Howard. May I present Mr. Peter Looney of Virginia? He needs a place to sleep until the stores open in the morning. Then I intend to see him dressed in clothes befitting a Colonial farmer."

"If you intend for him to stay in your room I'll have to charge you extra for the night."

"Add it to my bill, Mr. Howard." Holston turned away and Peter followed him up the stairs.

In Holston's room Peter saw something he hadn't seen in over a year; a bed, a table and a chair. "I feel like I've been away for half a lifetime." When he looked in the mirror he didn't recognize himself. "I reckon I do look like a Indian."

"We'll take care of that. I only have the one bed so . . ."

"I couldn't sleep in that anyway. I'll be just fine on the floor."

In the morning Peter awoke remembering where he was, and the taste of wonderful roasted beef eaten the evening before. As he lay on the floor staring at the tin ceiling with its elaborate designs he heard Holston wake up.

After a breakfast of eggs, bacon, bread and coffee Peter was led to the barbershop. "Our first order of business will be to do something with your hair." Inside the shop Peter was pleased to see it empty but for the barber. "My friend here needs to have something done with his hair."

"Is he an Indian?" The barber stared at Peter skeptically.

"No. He's a white man and we need to have him looking like one."

Holston took a chair by the window and watched as the barber began trimming Peter's hair.

"You're pretty well tanned Mr. . . . ."

"Looney. I be Peter Looney of Virginia. I be on my way back there as soon as Mr. Holston is finished making me look like what I be and not what I not be."

"I see," the barber smiled. "Well, that shouldn't be a problem. I'll leave enough so you can tie it behind in the fashion of the day."

"Much obliged."

"You have the accent of an Irishman, or is it British?"

"I not be either. Me Pa brought the family over in 1734 from the Isle-of-Mann, but I was the first of me brothers to be born in this country."

"Well, well, well. This is an interesting tid-bit I must add to the story," exclaimed Holston. "Now we need to get you dressed as the man we know you to be."

"I'm only a poor farmer." When Peter walked out of the clothing store he looked like other Colonials in Albany and with a full stomach, new clothes and tight shoes he stood on the sidewalk and smiled.

"It will take a day or so to get used to being dressed this way, but I'm beginning to feel like a white man again. It be a good feeling, and I can't thank you enough, Mr. Holston. Wish I could do something to repay you."

"You paid me last night with a wonderful story for my paper. By the way, you have a very long way ahead of you. He's some money you'll need for food, and I'll put you on the coach to New York. There's enough for the coach to Philadelphia as well. I'm afraid that's about all I can manage."

"All? That be more than enough. I thank ya kindly."

Chapter XXX

The easiest traveling Peter had ever known was the carriage ride from Albany to New York City. The realization that he could sit in a seat and look out a window while someone else drove the two horses was a revelation. He leaned back against the padded seat back and relaxed. The only thing wrong, and it took a few moments for him to understand, was the enclosed feeling. A coach was, after all a glorified box. He kept his face as close to the window as possible so he could breathe the air from outside. The only other passengers were two older women who seemed to prefer their own company and ignored Peter.

Just outside New York the coach came to a stop. "You have to get out here, Sir. They'll be another coach in the morning that can take you on to Philadelphia."

"You mean we'll be staying here tonight?" Peter got out and looked around. There was a gray stone building with a sign over the door. "Can I get something to eat here?" Other than a barn and a few out-buildings there was nothing else close by.

"Yes, Sir. It's an inn. They'll feed you and the ladies dinner and put you up for the night, for a fee of course."

"Of course." Peter walked into the main room that was empty but for an elderly couple.

"Good evening, Sir. Your dinner will be right out. Sit where ever you like." Peter chose a table in the corner where he could watch the door. The two women passengers chose a table at the other end of the room near a large stone fireplace. There was no fire and closed windows left the room very warm. It had been a hot day and the stone walls had retained the heat leaving the room stuffy. It was a square room with a set of stairs leading up to a second floor. The tables and chairs were made of heavy, rough hewed wood.

After a dinner of roasted chicken, bread with lots of gravy and a mug of beer, the owner approached Peter. "Do you want a bed for the night, Sir?"

"No. Beds be too soft. If ya don't mind I'd like to sleep here on the floor."

"On the floor? But, that's highly unusual."

"I know, but I been sleepin' on the ground so long that the floor will be just fine."

"Very well, but I need to charge you for the dinner."

Peter reached into his pocket and bull out one of the shillings that Mr. Holston had given him. He handed it to the owner not knowing if any change was due to him. "Thank you very much." He didn't think to ask the price of the meal ahead of time. The owner left and Peter sat cursing himself and vowed to be a little smarter next time. However, the owner returned a moment later and handed him four pence. Peter was relieved and smiled. "Thank you."

Bright and early the next morning a driver entered the inn and announced the coach for Philadelphia. This coach was more decorated than the one used the day before. The windows had curtains that could be closed on cold winter days. With the coach was a fresh team of horses. Three passengers climbed aboard, two men and a young woman. "Good morning to ya." He addressed the new passengers and tipped his hat to the young woman.

"Good morning, young man. How far will you be going this fine day?" He looked into the gray eyes of a well dressed man.

Peter smiled. The man was elegantly dressed in a fine gray wool coat with silver buttons and white lace trim at the throat and cuffs. The young woman was dressed in a suit of thin pale blue wool with a hat to match. He had to force himself to keep from staring at her. The jacket of her suit was nipped in at the waist and he was sure he had never seen such a tiny waist on a grown woman. He answered the man, "I'm taking this coach as far as Philadelphia, but my journey is to Virginia."

"Virginia? Would you by any chance know Governor Dinwiddie?"

Peter smiled openly, "No, Sir. Can't say I've had the pleasure. I been away for a little over a year, so I don't know any of the news."

"Well, I shall do my best to enlighten you. The British have begun a march to Fort Duquesne which they hope to take within the next few months. However, I just received word yesterday that Fort William Henry was taken and burned."

"That's terrible. I was traveling with a man I met in New York and he told me that Fort Oswego and Fort Ontario have been destroyed. How was Fort William Henry taken?"

"A Frenchman by the name of Montcalm had 12,500 Regulars and Indian Allies. The British held out for six days.[8] I fear we have not seen the end of this cursed war by any means. I'm on my way to Williamsburg. I hope to discuss matters with your governor. I've been hearing rumors of a young Colonel by the name of Washington. Do you know of him?"

"I've heard the name. The Indians have been very upset with him."

"I don't wonder. He was with Braddock. Let's see. Two years ago. Yes. Braddock may have been a superior General in Britain, but . . . ."

Peter could not refrain from interrupting this gentleman who had probably never been in battle, or on the far frontier. "He didn't understand how the Indians fight. It was a big mistake for him to assume the Indians are savages."

"You seem to be well informed on that subject. Why is that?" This stranger stared at Peter, but with his new clothes could not form an opinion.

"I lived with the Shawnee for a year. I ate with them, hunted with them. The chief had adopted me though I was a captive." The subject was becoming strained and Peter did not wish to continue with it. "Now, I only wish to return to my family in Augusta County."

"I wish you luck." The stranger was astute enough to see Peter's reluctance to continue.

"If you can bring an end to this war, I wish you luck." Peter stared out the window for the rest of the trip to Philadelphia.

Peter was unprepared for what he found there; too many people, and too much noise. Horses with and without carriages or wagons were in constant motion up and down the streets. He was surprised to find it larger than New York. Over the tops of buildings Peter saw the tall masts of sailing ships, and having never seen one, he decided to detour by way of the port.

It was late afternoon as he walked along the docks, busy with men loading or unloading wooden crates. The smell was a mixture of dead fish, polluted water and human waste. "This is not a nice place to be," he muttered as he shook his head. The desire to cover his nose was almost overwhelming, but he laughed silently to himself at what he might look like. *I look like a stranger to these parts, for sure.*

Finally, he stopped to stare at a large two-masted ship. *I reckon that's the kind of ship Pa brought the family over on.*

"You looking for somebody, mister?" Peter turned to see a small boy about nine years of age, barefoot with a worn shirt and rough knee length pants.

"No. I was just lookin'. I was thinkin' my Pa could a brought the family over on a ship like that one."

The boy looked at the ship sitting quietly on the water. "That be a English ship. Did you come from England?"

"No. My Pa came from the Isle-a-Mann."

"Never heard of that place. But, Sir, I'd be careful if I was you. It won't be safe to walk around the docks by yourself, especially after dark. The conscriptors be out lookin' for men like you to drag aboard British ships. Maybe, even that one."

"What exactly to you mean, little boy." Peter realized he didn't know anything about life in a port city. He didn't know about life in any city, for that matter, so he paid attention to the boy.

"They always need new men to work the ships. They're always short on sailors. They get lost at sea, or they run off as soon as the ship docks somewhere. Sometimes they just up and die cause it's so terrible on the ships. They usually take the drunk ones cause they can't fight so hard."

"Is life aboard one of those ships so bad as all that?"

"Yes, Sir. It be terrible. They beat you if you don't work hard enough, and the food ain't fit to feed a dog."

"How do you know all of this?" Peter stared at the boy who seemed to be about the same age as his youngest brother, Moses.

"My Pa told me. He sees 'em all the time. They hang out lookin' for men like you."

"Why like me?"

"Cause you look strong and healthy, and they figure they can get a lot of work out of you; that is before you die." The boy noted the surprise on Peter's face.

"That's pretty scary talk. How about you?"

"I'm too young now. But, before long I'll have to be careful or they'll get me too." The boy jumped up onto a box and started throwing stones into the water.

"I thank you for the warnin'. I'll be sure to be careful." Peter turned and left the boy standing on his box throwing stones. He walked further along the dock looking at other two -masted ships that sat side by side with schooners.

As the dock became shaded in the late afternoon Peter realized he'd better find a safe place to spend the night. The docks covered a large area, and as men left work for the day it became a lonely place. He continued walking south and before he reached the southern end of the docks he saw two men approach. *They be a mean lookin' pair, those do.* He quickly looked around and ducked between two buildings. The space was narrow but it led away from the docks. He hoped it would lead to a main street. The two men followed him. Peter ran. The two men ran after him. Peter turned the first corner, but it lead to a dead end between two warehouses. He had no choice but to turn and face the men who had followed him. He looked around for a weapon, a brick, a rock, a club, anything, but there was nothing.

"I guess you'll belong to us boyo."

"You sound Irish, like me. So what do you want?" Peter looked them straight in the eye, but he knew by the sneer on one man's face they would not be intimidated.

"I'm British ya bloody idiot. We were just thinkin' you'd make a fine sailor. Don't you think so Billy?"

"Sure do, Matt. What'a ya say, boy. Come along with us and enjoy the fine sea air."

"I thank you, kindly, but I've a mind to go home to Virginia."

"Virginia, is it? You're a far cry from home, sonny boy."

When the two men got close enough to jump him, Peter pulled off his hat and threw it into the face of one and jumped the other.

The punch to his stomach took the air out of Peter and he swung his fist into the chin of the nearest one as the other wrapped his arms around Peter pulling him to the ground. One fist landed in Peter's face just below his eye, and another in the chin. A third fist hit him in the stomach again. Peter fought as hard as ever, but the imbalance of power was taking its toll. Peter used everything he had, but not being very tall, his arms just didn't reach as far. He kicked, but so did they. Just as Peter was about to lose consciousness he heard shouting.

"Okay, you limies. Step aside. If you want a fight, we'd be more than happy to oblige ya." Two men jumped each of the men who had beaten up Peter. Then a few more men jumped in. The two conscriptors didn't have a chance. They fought hard to defend themselves as two or three sets of fists pounded them down onto the dirt.

In the meantime two men picked up Peter and carried him away. As Peter regained consciousness he yelled, "Let me be. I've no quarrel with you. Leave me alone." He struggled to free himself, but the arms that held him were strong.

"Relax, friend! We're on your side. Those blokes that beat you up are getting' what's due 'em. You come on back to the bar and we'll get you cleaned up a bit. You deserve a pint for the trouble they put you through."

"Let me down! Surely I can walk now."

"Okay." One man laughed as he helped Peter to his feet, but his legs gave out and they had to carry him back to the bar. "I didn't think you were up to walkin' just yet."

The owner of the bar saw them come in through the back door. "What are you doing?"

"Two limies were beatin' up this poor fella. Your Adam called us out, 'cause he figured what was going on. We need to clean him up."

"Looks like you need to wake him up. Come in. Lay him across a couple of chairs. I wondered why so many of you men ran out of here. I thought maybe there was a fire somewhere."

"No. Adam came a runnin'. He met this man earlier and knew he wasn't from around here. He seemed to be a likable sort o' feller, so he didn't want to see him conscripted to one of those British ships."

"Keep your voices down." The owner whispered harshly. "There's a lot of British in here and they may not take a liking to your language."

"Well, we don't take a liking to their means. Have Annie bring us a wet towel to wipe the blood off his face, so we can see what he looks like."

When Peter next opened his eyes he stared at a wooden ceiling and rough hewn beams and several heads hanging over him. He started to come up and fight his way out, but strong hands held him down. "You're safe now, my friend. No need to fight. I've ordered a pint for ya. That should bring you around."

Peter shook his head. "I thank ya for your care o' me, but I haven't had a pint of anything in over a year. Don't know that my stomach or my head can handle it."

"You don't drink? Better drink the pint, friend. The water is what'll make you sick."

"Where do you come from?" Several voices were all asking questions at the same time. Where did he come from? Why was he out there all alone?

"Let me sit up. I think I can handle that." Peter rose and sat on one of the chairs as the crowd of men gathered around him.

"That was a very satisfying fight we had. We haven't had any fun in a whole week."

"Yeah, it sure made me feel good to punch those two . . ." Someone poked the man in the ribs before he could say more.

Peter looked around him. His head hurt from the blows he had suffered. "How did you men know to come out there?"

"Little Adam. The owner's son said he met you earlier. When he saw those two men he figured out what was going to happen and came a runnin' to call us out. Nothing like a good fight to get the blood flowin'."

Another one spoke. "Yeah. It's a good thing for you Adam saw those men, or you'd be tied up aboard one o' those ships waitin' for it to sail. Once you're out to sea there ain't no turnin' back."

Peter looked past the group of men and saw a bright eyed little blond boy standing nearby. He reached out his hand to him. "Adam. You saved my life. I thank ya." The boy's father listened and then pulled the boy away.

"Okay, Adam. Off to bed with you."

The boy walked away a few steps, then turned and looked at Peter and smiled. Peter returned the smile, but grimaced from the pain.

"My jaw feels like I be kicked by a mule."

"You were, but the mule walked on two feet." Everyone roared with laughter. "Where's this man's pint of ale? Come on girl! Bring it here." A middle aged woman, with a rotund body and hair that had escaped from under her cap, carried a tray full of ale and sat it down on the table. Peter took the one handed to him. "Drink up boy. Then you can tell us why you were out there in the first place."

Peter took a sip and felt it begin to revive him. "I liked looking at the ships. I ain't never seen anything like it before. Me Pa brought the family over on such a ship before I was born. He landed here in Philadelphia."

"You say it was before you were born. What year would he have come over? And where from?" One of the men grabbed another mug and sat down across from Peter.

"He came in 1734 from the Isle-of-Mann. Me Ma says I was born in this town." Peter looked around, a bit curious as to who his benefactors were and why would they have bothered.

"Well, what'a ya know? He would have gone to Liverpool first to get a ship. By the way my name is Benjamin Murphy." He held out his hand and Peter took it.

"I don't know about that, but I reckon it could be."

"Where's your home?" Another asked.

"My home is in Augusta County, Virginia, between the Blue Ridge and the Allegany Mountains."

"You're a long way from home, son."

"I know, but I figure I'm about half way there from where I started. You see I was captured by the Shawnee and I lived with them for about a year. I was on a fur trading trip to Niagara and me and another white man escaped."

"Wow. Glad to see you got away from them savages."

Peter opened his mouth to defend the Shawnee, but changed his mind and remained silent. He would not have been able to change their opinions with only a comment or two.

"Now what are your plans?"

"I need to earn some money for food to carry with me on my way home."

"You ain't in no condition to work right now. You need a few days' rest. You can bunk in my room," Benjamin Murphy offered. "I work down the street at the feed store. I have a room up on the second floor over the store. You bunk with me while you mend."

"That's very kind of ya, Mr. Murphy." Peter tried to stand up, but found that a pint of ale on an empty stomach had the expected effect, and he staggered as he took a step.

"Hey, bar keep. I think this lad needs something solid in his stomach. How about a bowl of that stew you were serving earlier?"

"There's a little left, but who's going to pay for it?" The owner looked at Peter and though he sounded tough, he also had a soft spot for a fellow Manx-man. He did not tell them that though.

"Oh, come on. Do it for Adam's sake. Have a heart. Didn't you hear what he's been through?"

"I heard, but I don't need to be giving out free food to everybody who's had it rough."

"Pa, give it to him, please?" Adam had only gone up a few steps, but wanted to listen to the men.

"I told you to go to bed. Now, get." Darden turned half way toward his son and spoke harshly.

The boy only half listened. "Pa, please. He's a good man."

"What makes you such a judge of character?" The man sighed and knew he was going to give in to his only son.

"Please?"

"Oh, alright, but just this once. Now, go to bed." Mr. Darden looked down at his son, and though he would probably never show it, he was pleased with his son.

Peter gratefully accepted the bowl of stew, but thought that Red

Bird's stew tasted better. By the time he finished, the crowd had dispersed, and his new host escorted him to the room over the feed store. Aside from a man's smell there was the odor of various seeds, grains and hay from the store below.

"There's only the one bed, but I reckon it'll hold the two of us."

"I thank ya very kindly, but the floor be more to my likin'." Peter lay down, grateful to be in a prone position, and with a stomach full of stew and strong ale, he fell fast asleep.

Chapter XXXI

"Peter, wake up." His host, Ben Murphy called through a foggy cloud that enveloped Peter's mind. "Wake up. I have to go to work now. You stay here as long as you like. Okay?"

"Okay," Peter heard himself answer, and then everything went away and he was again asleep. Various noises infiltrated the small, quiet room from the street and from the feed store downstairs. Early dawn surrounded him and awakened the pain in his stomach, face and legs. Peter hurt in more places than ever in his life. By the afternoon he was aware of a change. It wasn't morning anymore. A strong ray of sunshine cut through the small room from the one window, and fell across Peter's chest. The noises from outside finally penetrated his consciousness. He opened his eyes. "Oh! Dear God, I hurt. Where am I?" He looked around and saw the small room with a bed, a table and one chair. Clothes were hanging on pegs that lined one wall. The floor was bare wood and he remembered the smells that came up from beneath the floor.

"Oh, god! Now I remember." He lifted himself onto one elbow and ran his hand over his face, lightly touching the swollen left eye. He pulled his hand away and saw a touch of blood on his finger tip. *There was a fight. People helped me and fed me.* He lay back and stared at the ceiling for a few minutes remembering all that had happened.

A man brought me to this room. What was his name? Ben something.

Irish name. Murphy. Yeah, that's it. Benjamin Murphy. That be the feed store downstairs. Peter rolled to his side and groaned. *I think I'll rest a minute more.*

"Hello, Peter." Murphy came up the stairs to the room and found Peter where he had left him that morning. "Are you feelin' any better, Peter?"

"I think I'll live. Many thanks to you and your friends."

"Do you think you can get up and walk?" Murphy held out a hand and helped Peter to his feet. "That be some shiner those guys gave you. If you can manage I'll buy you somethin' to eat. I know you said you didn't have any money. So, I don't mind helping a fellow Irishman."

"If I can find some work I will gladly repay you for all you've done."

"Don't think about that right now. Come on. A good meal will go a long way to making you feel better." Peter got to his feet and was surprised that in spite of his pain he actually could walk.

At the bar Peter recognized a few of the faces from the past evening. "Hey, here comes our friend. I'd recognize you anywhere by the cuts on your face, and the black eye."

Peter gave them a painful smile. "I think one of those must 'a been usin' somethin' metal to make so many cuts on my face."

"You're right." One of the men held out a metal ring. "Found it on one of those blokes that jumped you last night. I make it a present to you."

Peter shook his head. "Maybe you should keep it to use against one of those guys next time." The man smiled and slipped it into his pocket.

By the time Peter and his new friend, Ben Murphy finished dinner and downed a few ales Peter had two possible job offers. "I don't know how I can thank you lads."

"Stick around town for awhile," Timothy Morgan suggested. Tim worked for the shoemaker and had suggested he try his hand. "Everybody needs shoes sooner or later. I'll talk to my boss in the morning. After all you said you used to make your own moccasins. There's probably not that big a difference."

"Your boss may differ with you," Peter smiled in gratitude.

"I'll talk to the owner of the feed store. I know you can carry bags of grain and seed," added Murphy.

"He's got to heal up before somebody has him lifting those heavy sacks of grain." Another man, Martin Alexander joined in.

"You gents are shore mighty good to me." Peter sipped his pint of ale, feeling it slide down his throat, but making his head a bit dizzy.

"Why not? Last night was mighty entertaining." Alexander smiled. "It really got my blood boilin'. I'd fight for money if there was anybody to pay me for it." Alexander then laughed heartily. "Well, anyway, those blokes had it comin' to 'em. I've heard tell of too many good men carted off by them, never to be seen again on these shores."

Peter looked at Alexander, wondering if he was joking or not. He was a big, burly sort of man, with red hair and broad shoulders. Peter had no doubt he'd win most any fight he cared to enter.

The next morning Peter met Timothy Morgan at the bar where they had breakfast and walked down the street a block to the shoemaker's shop where Timothy worked. The owner of the shop, a German named Ebert Ellrodt watched Timothy as he entered the shop.

"You bring me a customer, and so early today." He smiled and held out his hand to Peter.

"I'm sorry, Mr. Ellrodt. This is Peter Looney. He needs a job. He's made plenty of Indian moccasins, and I thought you could use an extra pair of hands for awhile."

"Moccasins are not like shoes. Shoes must be made a certain size for each customer."

"If you would allow me to work for you, Sir, I promise to learn the difference very quickly. I be good with my hands, and they be one part of me that didn't get beat up by a couple of British thugs having their hearts set on me joinin' their ship."

"Conscriptors?" Mr. Ellrodt looked at the black eye Peter was now wearing. "Looks like they worked you over."

"Yes, sir, but Timothy and some other men saved me. I wish to work and earn enough money to repay them for all they've done."

"Well. Business has been pretty good lately. Soldiers have been coming through needing boots and shoes to replace the ones they wear out on those marches to where ever the fighting is. So, I'll want you to promise me you'll stay around long enough to be of use to me after you've learned how to make a decent pair of boots. Otherwise, I'd have no use for you."

"I promise, you'll not be sorry." Peter stood ramrod straight and held out his hand.

"Promises, promises. Okay, Peter Looney. Let's see what you can do."

At the end of the day, Mr. Ellrodt asked, "where about are you laying you head at night?"

"I don't really have a place. Another kindly gent let me sleep on the floor in his room, but that was only for two nights. I can't afford a hotel room."

"There a spot in the back room. You can sleep there if you don't mind crates, and barrels and stuff."

"I wouldn't mind at all. I'm used to sleepin on the ground."

"Well, this isn't much better, but you'll have a roof over your head. I'll have to give you a key to the shop so you can get in after you've had your supper."

Mr. Ellrodt handed a key to a very grateful Peter and together they walked out of the shop with Timothy. The shoe shop owner walked one way and Peter and Timothy went to the bar where they met others for their supper. Peter hadn't had a job that paid anything since cutting logs to build a fence for James Patton, one of those killed at Draper's Meadow.

The following week Peter met his new friends in the bar. "Okay, men. I've received my first pay, so I can repay the kindness of feeding me all this past week. First I owe Ben three dinners, and then I owe Tim three dinners. Then I owe . . ."

"If you insist on paying each of us by buying us dinners, we'll accept, but then you'll have to stay another week to save up for your trip."

"You're right. I hadn't looked at it that way. And if I pay you in cash money I won't have enough left. So, I guess I'll have to stay another week." Peter was glad that he was able to repay his new friends, but he did long to be on his way. It was still summer and his chances of getting home before fall were still good.

"Good. Let's drink to that. Hey barkeep. Six ales."

Peter ended up staying two additional weeks in order to save enough money. When it was time to leave he said all his goodbyes after dinner and waited for the shoe shop owner, Mr. Ellrodt to come into the store. "Mr. Ellrodt. I want to thank ya for allowin' me to work for ya. I couldn't leave without tellin' you that, and I needed to return the key you kindly let me use."

"You got a very long way to go yet, Peter. Are you sure you will be okay?"

Peter's smile covered his face, now healed from the beating he endured. "I figure I be half way there from where I started. I've no fear I'll make it the rest of the way. But, I thank you for your carin'."

"Goodby, Peter. Maybe you can use your new skills when you get back home. People always need shoes."

"Thank ya kindly, Mr. Ellrodt."

A few miles south of Philadelphia he came to a fork in the road.

A farmer was pulling a wagon along the road. "Sir, could you tell me where that road over there goes?"

"That road goes around the city of New York. You ever been there?"

"No. I'm on my way to Virginia and I'd just as soon stay away from any cities."

"Son, you don't know what you're missing, but hop into the back of my wagon. I can take you a little ways along that road. At least you won't have to walk all the way."

"Thank you kindly." Peter hoped into the back of the man's wagon. Next to him were cages of chickens, and one duck. *I reckon he's a farmer from the looks of the wagon and the way he was dressed.* The man was indeed a farmer, and sucked on a cold pipe stem as he spoke to his one horse, a gray mare that seemed too old to be pulling a wagon. The horse plodded along the road so slowly Peter was sure he could walk as fast. However, it gave his feet a rest from the tight shoes he was given by the newspaper man in Albany.

Aside from the shoes that weren't going to last much longer, Peter's new white shirt was mended after being torn in the fight, his pants were missing one bucket below the left knee and the stockings had holes in them. His hair was tied in back with a new ribbon and he still had the tri-corner hat that came with the new clothes.

The farmer left Peter at the side of the road and pointed him in the direction he needed to go. Then he directed his horse down a one lane path and disappeared among the trees.

"Well, I be on me own again and nobody to talk to. I didn't think I'd miss the company of those fellers in Philadelphia, but at least I learned something about shoe making. Pa will be happy to know that. Of course I'll have to get the tools from Williamsburg, but I reckon we can work out something. Well, at least it be a clear sky and a fine breeze. A good day for travelin'."

The only thing Peter carried was a sack of bread and cheese to eat along the way plus some money saved from working. "With a little money to jingle in me pocket I feel like a rich man."

He walked along the road during the day, but at night slept in the woods out of sight. Three days later he crossed a clear creek and using a little bar of soap he had purchased he washed his clothes and bathed in the shallow water. He spread out his clothes and lay on a grassy patch while his clothes dried in the sun. He put his hands behind his head and relaxed as he contemplated his circumstances.

"If it was a little later in the season I could hunt for berries and nuts in the woods. I'd best be careful and not eat all my food. I got to make it last as long as possible. I left Philadelphia on the fifteenth of August, so by my reckoning it's the twentieth now. Nothing will be ready for pickin' for another month and sure hope to be home by then."

He put his shirt in the sack he carried. "Maybe I can keep it clean if I don't wear it. Peter's year with the Indians had altered his perception of propriety. "I hope nobody mistakes me for an Indian being without a shirt, but I don't carry any markings of an Indian. That shirt be too close to me. I don't like it now, though I had to abide by it while I was livin' in the city. Maybe there be no more cities I have to go through."

Another day and he approached a wide river. "If this be the Potomac, Virginia be on the other side. This be a rough place to cross." All along the river from where he stood were sheer cliffs on either side that rose a good hundred feet, topped by forest. "I can't cross here. I hope I don't have to walk too far upriver to find a good fordin' place." Unfortunately, Peter walked all the rest of that day and part of the following morning. There was no ferry and the river was too wide for a bridge, so Peter put his pants in the cloth bag with his shirt, shoes and socks. "Maybe my hat stay on my head whilst I swim across." Near the shore he saw geese and a few ducks floating along in the calmer parts and decided the water was calm enough. The countryside was devoid of people, and he traveled south eventually finding a road that ran north-south. Once a day he found a tavern and after three days without food he decided to venture inside.

"I'd like to buy some bread and meat or cheese to carry with me."

"You might find the meat difficult to carry and I don't have any cheese. I can sell you a loaf of bread for six pence."

"Isn't that a pretty high price for one loaf."

"Take it or leave it." The proprietor stared at him.

Peter knew he only had a few shillings left, but he bought the bread anyway and left. "That man be a robber, and this bread not worth more than three pence. Best be more careful."

"I'll surely not find work in this country. Most everybody has slaves to do their work and those that don't are too poor to give away food they need for their own."

That night as Peter found a comfortable spot among a cluster of trees it began to rain. Lightning and thunder made sleep impossible. He put his shirt back on and hid his sack under some brush hoping it wouldn't get wet. "The shirt won't keep me dry, but the heavy drops be hittin' the shirt and not me bare skin." He stood up and moved closer to a larger tree with full branches. He looked up through the leaves as lightning struck another tree not ten feet from him. Peter was knocked down by the blast and lay unconscious for several minutes as rain pelted him.

When he regained consciousness he quickly got to his feet. "I best get away from here, but where?" In the distance he saw a barn. *I'd best get inside that barn. Maybe the people won't do me any harm considering the storm.* He grabbed his sack and ran, not knowing how long he had lain on the ground. He climbed over two fences to reach the barn. "It's dark in here." He had to use his sense of smell and touch to find a dry, clean spot of hay to lie on. He crept along the wall and felt for the stalls, being as quiet as he possibly could. *This hay smells fresh.* He lay down on the warm dry hay and fell fast asleep.

"Hey you. What are you doin' in this here barn? You best get outta here fore the boss man find you. He whip you good."

Peter opened his eyes to find a black slave dressed in nothing more than ragged pants standing over him and holding a pitch fork. "I'm sorry." He jumped up and moved toward the door. "I was in the woods last night but lightning struck a tree and knocked me out. I needed shelter from the storm. I'm leaving."

"It don't matter to me. It's the boss man you gotta watch out fir. You best hurry."

Peter ran and as he crossed over the second fence he cursed himself. "My sack. Damn. I left my sack in the barn." He stopped at the side of the road and looked back. "I'm glad I ate some of that bread last night. I reckon the rest of it be a mess now anyway. Oh well. I slept good on that straw."

Peter walked from one farm to another, passing the occasional tavern. The humid heat of August beat down on him from sun up to sun down as he trudged on with bare feet growing tough as shoe leather. At another tavern he bought bread and a little meat. He sat under a big oak tree that night and ate heartily. "That be the best meal I've had in many a day. I'll leave some for tomorrow."

He found a farmer out in a field and he called to him. "Hey, mister. What be that town up ahead?"

"Stauton. That be the next town."

When he arrived there were only a few houses, a stable, a general store, a hardware and feed store combined, but little else. "Maybe the general store also sells food."

"Good afternoon, Sir. What do you charge for one loaf of bread?"

"Don't sell bread. Folks around here make their own." The owner stared at Peter but didn't move a muscle.

"Do you have any cheese?" Peter looked hopeful and a little worn out.

"Never carry cheese. Sorry, young man. I got tobacco and dried beans and such."

"Thank you," and Peter left. He had no way of cooking beans.

Now, I be in a heap of trouble. One shilling and three pence left and no food to buy." Peter walked for another three days with nothing to eat. That evening he spotted a small grove of apple trees and hid in the bushes until dark. He picked as many as he could carry. "They not be ripe yet, but I be a poor beggar, in no position to be choosey." He ate hungrily as he walked and after eating four of the green apples he realized his mistake.

He grabbed his stomach and headed for a wooded area and hid among the bushes being sick. "Ma always told me never to eat a apple 'fore it's time. But I be too hungry to care." Peter lay there for the rest of the night and most of the next day.

When Peter finally felt well enough to walk he went back to the road. With a belly ache that was impossible to ignore he trudged on, sitting down every now and then to rest. "I might as well just stay here a while. I feel so rotten and I make no progress. Ma, I'll never doubt ya again."

This time he lay down on the side of the road under a small tree that allowed so little shade he had to move as the sun moved. But after awhile he fell asleep.

"Mister? What you doin' layin' there like you be dyin or somethin'?"

"Maybe I am, and maybe I don't care at this moment." Peter looked up into the face of a young black woman in a plain blue dress.

"Lordy be. You come with me. My mistress give you sompin' to eat. She don't hold to denying a man food if'n he needs it. I guess you ain't got any money?"

"I have one shilling three pence left. I'll gladly pay for a loaf of bread if you got it."

"Ain't no never mind. She feed you for free." She helped him to his feet and walked with him down a side road to the front of a large white house. A porch ran the length of the house and columns rose to the top of the second floor. The house was surrounded by tall oak trees and all but invisible from the main road. "You sit right here while I talk to the mistress."

Peter lay in the shade of the porch and was almost asleep when an elderly woman approached and looked down at him. "Young man. What is your name and where are you from?"

"Hello, ma'am. My name is Peter Looney. My home is just south of the James River. I've been away for over a year and I'm trying to get home."

"Why is it you have no money or horse?"

"I had a horse before I was captured by the Indians last year, but they took it. I escaped about two months ago. I stayed in Philadelphia three weeks to earn enough money for food, but now I'm down to one shilling three pence. I would gladly pay you for a little food."

"You were captured by the Indians?"

"Yes ma'am."

"You poor man. Mindy, help me get him into the kitchen. After we get you fed you'll have to rest awhile. I'll get you some clean clothes too."

"Just a little food would be appreciated." Peter felt so out of place in such a nice house, one almost as nice as Sir William Johnson. Of course, he could only imagine what that one looked like. This one was so fine he dared not touch anything.

"Nonsense. You need more than just a little food."

After eating, Miss Evelyn Warren showed him to a room at the back of the house. "You lie down and sleep. You're much too worn out to travel anywhere today."

"You're very kind but . . ."

"No buts. You need to rest. We'll talk later." Peter looked at the feather bed covered with pillows and a brightly colored quilt. He walked over to it and pushed his hand down, feeling the softness of the feathers. He smiled, "I ain't never slept on anything that soft." There was a rug on the floor so he lay down on it and soon was fast asleep.

"Mindy, has our guest awakened?"

"No mistress. But I peeked in a' he was sleepin' on the floor. He never even touched the bed."

"Well, I suppose he got used to sleeping on the ground while he was a captive of those heathens."

"Yes, mistress. Does you want me to wake him for supper?"

"Yes, we need to put more meat on those bones. He looks much too thin. It's a wonder all that walking hasn't made him ill."

A day later Peter was sitting on the front porch dressed in good, clean clothes. "Miss Warren. You've been more than generous to me. But, these clothes must belong to someone who will miss them."

"No. They were my nephew's. He was in the militia and was killed by the Indians two years ago. He would want you to have them. He would have been just a little older, I think, but I'm glad to see them put to good use." Miss Warren waved her fan in front of her face and sat quietly rocking in her chair. Peter leaned against one of the columns along the porch and listened to the rocker as it squeaked quietly over the wooden planking.

"I'm sorry about your nephew. My oldest brother was also killed. He was buried along Reed Creek. He was on a mission against the Indians."

"Too many people have died defending our farms."

Peter wanted to tell her that this land belonged to the Indians before the white men came, but he couldn't. "Yes ma'am. I reckon more will die before we make peace. First we have to take the land back from the French who pay the Indians to kill the whites."

"I pray every day that peace will come." Miss Warren touched her scented handkerchief to her noise.

"Yes ma'am. Now, I reckon you'd like to see the back of me, so I'll be leaving first thing in the morning."

"I'll hear no such thing, young man. You have worn yourself to skin and bone. You need more rest. So don't you go runnin' off before you're well enough."

"You are very kind, but I think I will be well enough."

"No you won't. You promise me you'll stay at least two more days. Promise me."

Peter did not want to offend the woman's kindness and she was probably lonely without her nephew. "Yes, ma'am. I promise." Those two days were probably the most leisure Peter had known since leaving the Shawnee village.

When the day came for Peter to leave, he stood on the front porch with her trying to say goodbye. Miss Warren's slave, Mindy came around from behind the house leading a horse. "Peter, I want you to take this horse."

"But, Miss Warren."

"I'll hear no buts from you young man. I have other horses, and

I've little use for this one. As you can see he's a bit old. He hasn't many years left. I was going to let him retire to the field, but I think he will see you to your home."

"I seem to keep thankin' you. You been so generous; I really can't say it enough. But, one more time, thank you.

"God speed you on your way. I've enjoyed your visit here."

Peter waved goodbye and turned to face the horse. The saddle was an old one, but he hadn't been in a saddle since his capture. He spoke to the horse. "I wonder if you belonged to the nephew that was killed. These stirrups fit like they were made for me. Well, horse. She didn't tell me your name, but I reckon we'll be friends for the rest of my journey, or until you wear out."

Back on the porch Miss Warren and Mindy stood watching as Peter rode away. "Miss Warren. We gonna miss that nice young man."

"Yes, Mindy, we will miss him. For a few short days it was like having my nephew Peter at home again."

"Yes'm, it was."

After two days of easy riding storm clouds began to form. The air was humid and growing cooler. The clouds grew heavier and darker as the wind began to blow.

"I sure don't like the looks of those clouds. Reckon we be in for another rain storm. I can smell it in the air. Sure would hate to mess up these nice clothes Miss Warren give me."

Along the main road that ran down the Shenandoah Valley were more farms, poor cabins and occasionally a barn. He rode up to one of the better cabins and asked for shelter until the rain stopped.

"My name be Peter Looney, Ma'am. And I was wondering would you mind if I sat out this rain on your porch here or in your barn? I been travelin' a long way and hate to get these fine new clothes all wet."

"Peter Looney? Is your Pa Robert Looney down south o' the James?" When he heard his father's name he opened his mouth and stared. It took a moment for him to answer.

He shook his head as the let the sound penetrate. "Yes. You know my Pa?"

"I hear talk of him now and again. He operates the ferry, don't he? Got a right good size orchard too."

"That he does."

"Well, Mr. Looney, you come on in and rest a spell. That storm might hang around too long. It could be a bad one."

"Thank you. What about my horse? I don't reckon a little rain would hurt him, but he's getting on in years so I'm sure he'd rather not."

"Johnny, go put this man's horse in the barn." She turned and spoke to a young boy of about eight who was hiding behind her skirts.

"I'll be getting' ya a drink of water if you like."

"That'll be fine, Mrs. . . ."

"Mabel Smith. My husband's out back in the barn. He'll be mighty pleased to make your acquaintance." She disappeared and shortly returned with a cup of water.

"Thank you, Mrs. Smith."

"Oh shucks, call me Mabel. Everybody else does. You must be on your way back home."

"I am. I've been away for over a year."

"I done hear folks talk about that. You and Captain Smith and a bunch of other folks captured by the Indians. I heard about a party that tried to follow but they didn't come back with anybody."

"That's a shame. Levisa Vause wrote her name on trees as far north as the Ohio River, but I guess that's where he lost the trail."

"Your folks are gonna be mighty pleased to know you're still alive. Land a Goshen, what a story you got to tell." She grabbed both of her hands and pulled them to her chest as her eyes lit up.

"Mr. Looney. Adam Smith. Hear you're on your way back home after being captured by the Indians. Did they treat you okay, or did they make you a slave?"

"I was treated well. It's good to meet you, Mr. Smith." Peter stuck out his hand. "Your wife was kind enough to let me sit out the storm here where it's nice and dry."

"That storm might stick around 'til after dark. The thunder's pretty loud. Mabel we'll have a guest for supper. Hope you can stay, Mr. Looney. You don't want to be out when it's lightening and thundering like it is."

"That's mighty kind of you." Peter enjoyed a home cooked meal much like those he remembered his mother making. And for the first time in over a year he ate an apple dumpling.

Later, when he laid down on the floor to sleep he stared at the rough hewn ceiling timbers and listened to the dying thunder as it rumbled away towards the northeast. His visit with this family, though strangers, was almost like being home. His heart ached to see his mother and father, his brothers and two sisters. He was so close; he felt the familial ties growing tighter.

The next morning the sun grew bright in a clear and cloudless sky. Peter was eager to leave, knowing he was close to home. "Thank you for a wonderful supper and breakfast. But, I have one question. How far do you reckon it is to the James River?"

"You're very close now. I figure maybe twenty miles. You'll be slee-pin' at your Pa's place tonight."

"Those are wonderful words to hear. Thank you again, and good-bye."

The horse had become a companion, someone Peter could talk to, and he did. "I like to cried when that man said I'd be home by night-fall." He tried singing a song, but his singing was no better than his whistling. The horse whinnied. "I think I'll have to give you a name. I don't like calling you horse. How about Thunder? Yeah. That's it." He leaned forward and patted the horse's neck. Thunder whinnied. "I take that to mean you agree."

As much as Peter wanted to gallop the rest of the way he was afraid to push the poor old horse too hard for fear it would collapse along the way. He had no desire to do injury to the horse. As he rode south along the Great Wagon Road he watched the shadows and kept looking toward the hills far off to the west. By afternoon, their shapes began to look familiar and he knew he was getting close to the James River and home. Then he began to pass cabins that belonged to people he knew. Just north of the James River he crossed through land purchased by James Patton who had been killed by the Indians at Draper's Meadow two years earlier.[9].

At the river he whistled. A boy came out and saw a rider on a brown gilding. Peter watched his youngest brother, Moses, pull the ropes that guided the ferry across the river. It was no more than a large raft but big enough to hold a wagon and two horses. A rope was threaded through two posts, forming a loop from shore to shore. The ferryman pulled the raft across the river in a straight path. A pull on the other part of the looped rope would send it back to the other side. Peter dismounted and walked the horse onto the raft and kept his head down just enough that the tri-cornered hat covered his eyes. As he walked the horse off the ferry he looked straight into Moses's eyes and smiled a broad and happy smile. His heart filled with joy at seeing his youngest brother.

"Hello, little bro. My but you done growed up. I almost don't recognize you."

The boy looked up and seeing his missing brother began to shout. "Peter! It's Peter!" Moses yelled back to the house as the two of them hugged and Peter picked up Moses and swung him around. "Ma! Pa! Peter's come home."

The two walked up toward the house as his mother and father rushed out the door followed by Joseph and John all calling his name at once. Peter hugged his mother, then his father and two brothers.

"Peter! Peter! We were so afraid we'd never see you again." His mother's tears rolled down her face as she held him tight, reluctant to let go.

"It's good to be home." Peter held onto his mother and kissed her on both cheeks.

"Come in. Moses, put the horse in the barn. Peter, you have to tell us everything. Where did they take you? How did they treat you? Did any of the others come back with you?"

"Ma. Pa. One question at a time." Peter looked from one to the other grinning from ear to ear.

"Where did you get those fancy clothes? Did you steal 'em off somebody's clothesline?" Joseph laughed as he poked Peter gently on the arm.

"They were given to me by a very nice lady whose nephew was killed two years ago."

"Oh." Suddenly everyone stopped talking at once, and their mood turned solemn.

"I guess you'll want your old bed back. Moses been sleepin' there but we'll put a pallet on the floor."

Peter laughed. "Ma. I'll sleep on the pallet. I haven't slept in a bed in over a year. I tried once, but it was too soft. I can sleep on a rug, on the ground, but not in a bed. Moses, you don't have to give up your bed for me."

"What happened to the other captives? We were told there were twenty-four of you. Did they stay with you?"

"No. There were about four different tribes in the raid, and once they took us north of the Ohio they divided us up. Charlotte Vause and Sarah Medley stayed at the lower Scioto River village with the Shawnees. Also Vause's slave, Tom. He was adopted."

"I talked to Vause when he got back. He said he saw Charlotte and Sarah, but Charlotte wouldn't come back. He said they had been adopted and the Indians wouldn't let them go."

"Yes, they were. Sarah got used to the Shawnee ways pretty fast. I don't know where the rest of 'em went except for Captain Smith. He was turned over to the French in Detroit and I heard he was taken to Canada. I don't know any more about him. They took me to Detroit, but I was adopted by one of the chiefs as his brother. He treated me very well. I learned a lot. I'm good with a bow and arrow now, and I'm better at skinning animals. Men don't do anymore than that. The rest is women's work." He winked at his mother.

"I hope you don't think I'll be tanning hides." Peter's mother exclaimed as she stood up to put more stew in his bowl.

Everyone talked until the wood in the fireplace had turned to embers. In the morning Moses rode out to pass the word to the rest of the family that Peter was home.

Peter stood at the doorway breathing in the fresh air of southwest Virginia and looking west toward the mountains he had walked across the year before. "Pa. I should go talk to Mr. Vause. I want to tell him what I know about his family. It's not much, but I think he'd want to know."

"Ephraim Vause sold his land and moved north not a month after returning from that rescue trip. He was a broken man, Peter."

"I'm sorry to hear that. Loss of loved ones hits us all pretty hard."

"You talk like you know something about that."

Peter didn't answer his father, but went outside to walk through the family's fields. The fort his father built had never been damaged by an Indian attack. The fields were full and green. The corn was high, waving in the breeze. The orchards were full of fruit not far from being ripe. It was a beautiful sight. Peter walked down to the river and sat on the grass. "No rock here to sit on while rapids roll over other rocks. No Nuttak." Every emotion returned as he remembered the events of his last year. Remembering Nuttak was the most difficult of all. He tried to fight back the tears but finally let them fall, as he thought about the only woman he had ever loved.

END NOTES

1 The first names of Graham and Cole are not known. These are fictional.

2 Draper's Meadow is the site where another Mary Ingles, sister-in-law to the one mentioned here was captured in May 1755. She later escaped from Bone Lick, Kentucky and made her way home.

3 It is still called Abb's Valley today, and all the inhabitants were wiped out by the Indians in 1755. Absalom Looney had moved back to the family farm in order to help his father build Looney's fort. After Fort Vause was destroyed Looney's fort became the most western fort on the frontier.

4 This wording was taken from an old hymn book left by my mother.

5 Peter did meet a William Phillips while at Niagara. They escaped together.

6 This is true according to Peter's testimony.

7 Peter really was interviewed by a reporter for the London Chronicle. This was later reprinted.

8 In 1758 the tide turned when Brigadier General John Forbes and 6,000 men from Fort Cumberland marched to Fort Duquesne, but leaving in the summer he worked his way slowly and the fort wasn't taken until winter.

9 The Draper's Meadow massacre was where Mary Ingles and her sister-in-law, Betty Draper were captured. We don't know what happened to Betty, but Mary escaped and barely made it back alive.

Bibliography   Below is a partial listing of sources

Derounian-Stofola, Kathryn Zabelle, *Women's Indian Captivity Narratives*, Penguin Books, NY, 1998.

Drimmer, Frederick, editor, *Captured by the Indians*, 15 Firsthand Accounts, 1750-1870, Dover Publications, Inc., NY, 1961.

Eckert, Allan W., *That Dark and Bloody River*, Bantam Books, 1995.

Eckert, Allan W., *The Frontiersmen*, Little, Brown & Co., 1967.

Eckert, Allan W., *Wilderness Empire*, Jesse Stuart Foundation, Ashland, Kentucky, 2001

Gilbert, Bil, *God Gave Us This County*, Doubleday, New York, 1989.

Greene, Evarts Boutell, *The Foundations of American Nationality*, American Book Company, New York; Cincinnati, 1922.

Kennedy, Billy, *Women of the Frontier*, Ambassador Emerald International, Greenville, South Carolina, 2004

Kincaid, Robert L., *The Wilderness Road*, Bobs-Merrill, Indianapolis, 1947.

Leyburn, James G., *The Scotch-Irish: A Social History*, University of North Carolina Press, Chapel Hill, NC, 1962.

Morris, Michael P., *The Bringing of Wonder: Trade and the Indians of the Southeast, 1700-1783*, Greenwood Press, Westport, CT, 1999.

Rutman, Darrett Bruce, *A Place in Time*, W. W. Norton & Co., New York, 1984.

Summers, Lewis. P., *History of Southwest Virginia, 1746-1786, Washington County, 1777-1870*, Genealogical Publishing Company, Baltimore, MD, 1966. (reprint of an originally published book 1903)

Wertenbaker, Thomas J., *The Shaping of Colonial Virginia*, Russell & Russell, New York, 1958.

Wokeck, Marianne S., *Trade in Strangers: The Beginnings of Mass Migration to North America*, Pennsylvania State University Press, University Park, PA. 1999.

Wright, Louis B., *Life on the American Frontier*, A Perigee Book, G. P. Putnam's Sons, New York, 1968.

www.looneybook.com

www.nationalregisterofhistoricplaces.com